*IN LOVING MEMORY OF GRANDMA GLADYS, WHO
LOVED EVERYTHING ABOUT CHRISTMAS*

DR. CHRISTMAS

Prologue

DECEMBER 24, 1998

As the Santa Ana winds chilled the starless December night's air, the homes of slumbering residents that nestled in a quiet suburban San Bernardino Valley neighborhood blended into the darkness, like a piece of monochromatic artwork of both man-made and God-created structures against the warm black sky.

While brief power outages were common during this time of year, what was uncommon to the inhabitants of this particular cul-de-sac, was what had transpired undetected, but witnessed only by the secret-keepers of the shadows.

It was just moments before the town's grid reset, when there was an ultrabright amber flash casting a glow upon the doorstep of one quaint Tudor-style home in Fontana, California. A sudden short gust of wind followed, then a chime of jingling bells could be heard, awakening the canine ears in proximity. A symphony of barking dogs began to sound as nature paid homage to the essence of magic lingering in the air by hiding all but the dance of the hem of a red velvet cape scurrying away from the property as the electricity was restored.

The twinkling Christmas lights that donned every abode surrounding this dormant quiescent home that lacked any festive holiday décor year after year, illuminated and bedazzled the dark sky resembling an aurora of northern lights over the valley.

Upon this home's doorstep emerged a large wicker basket with a thick wool red and black buffalo-patterned blanket covering its sporadically moving content, causing a string of bells to ring again.

The window drapes appeared to move along the outer edge of the window shortly before a dimly lit interior lamp came on. The door slowly opened, but only partially ajar, revealing 2 sets of bare feet and four dancing sandy blonde paws.

With one more jingle, the door opened wider, and the basket was lifted, disappearing into the house where almost instantly a bigger amber glow could be seen through every covered window of the home for a flash of a second from the outside, but lasted for several enchanted Christmas Eve minutes within.

CHAPTER ONE

SPECIAL DELIVERY

TWENTY-SEVEN YEARS LATER...

The bell sounded signaling the end of the yoga exercise routine, and of course, she did one additional deep-breathing repetition before opening her eyes, because no matter what was expected, Kristina did at least one more of anything; because that is just what overachievers do.

Placing her fingertips against her carotid artery, she was satisfied with her resting heart rate and rose to her feet and released her tightly twisted bun from the clutch of a violet scrunchie that matched her purple ombré yoga pants. Her wavy auburn hair fell upon her shoulders as she combed her fingers through it to allow the air to flow against her damp scalp.

Kristina, 26 placed her lunch order from her tablet while snuggled up in her favorite high-armed chair that cradled her like the oversized giant teddy bear; Theodore, that she slept with as a child. The teddy bear that still sits on her childhood bed awaiting her now infrequent visits home.

Kristina took a moment to ponder and analyze the challenge that she received from a few of her peers earlier in the week on improving a work-life balance. Specifically, to take time to smell the roses. She was determined to actually relax on her day off from her hectic hospital rotation week, she just could not think of balancing an almost non-existent outside-of-work life.

Although beautiful, brilliant, and accomplished, Kristina was still single with no suitors. She has been giving herself the same internal speech as a daily affirmation since breaking up with her High School boyfriend 2-months before prom and graduation, and certainly after the 2 blind dates in college that she never gave a call back. Even now with most of her career goals met, she continues to tell herself that she did not have the time or energy to nurture an emotionally needy companion that would require her to deviate from her normal day-to-day routine. Her strict LA dating rules of no co-workers, no colleagues, no neighbors, no social media dating, and absolutely no professional athletes or celebrities left the designed dating pool rather sparse.

With both knees against her chest and her toes digging into the chair cushion, she peered out of the sliding glass door to her balcony to take in the city views that she normally would ignore on her way in or out to work. Kristina inhaled deeply as she stared out from her contemporary NoHo high-rise apartment onto the densely populated valley and the sun-kissed mountain skyline.

She allowed herself to savor a sense of accomplishment as nesting in Los Angeles, the city of dreams, was right on schedule in her planned trajectory. And so was an early entrance to Med School and completing her residency before her 27th birthday, which was now just a month away. But in the normal

Kristina fashion, she always had a new goal in the wind as she approached the finish line of another goal. She embraced immersing herself in the diverse culture of LA. Even though work, community interests, and charity participation kept her busy; for Kristina, inner fulfillment has never been achieved. For reasons unknown to her, she simply could never shake the feeling of incompleteness. It was an overwhelming sensation that she endured even as a child that became the motivation for the manner in which she pursued her dreams and career endeavors well into adulthood.

Breaking her concentration was the familiar ring tone of an upbeat melody designated to her top three contacts. Kristina welcomed the distraction as she reached for her cellphone.

"Heyyy," cheerfully greeted Kristina.

"Hey yourself. So, who is the best publicist and best friend ever?"

"Oh London, you are of course! Is that a rhetorical question?"

"I just heard back from the network and Tina; you are practically a shoo-in for next season's cast."

"Practically?" she questioned in a more solemn tone.

"Well, you know how it is in Hollywood, the offer isn't inked yet, but minor details. I tell you, girlfriend, they really want you."

"Hmm, so you keep saying London, but…"

"But nothing. Number one, you are gorgeous. Your audition tapes...amazing! The camera loves you!

Number two, your second book, Designer Babies, has been on the best Seller's list for eight weeks now."

"Nine, but who's counting?"

"We both are, my friend," London giggled. "Don't give up hope. To be the first and only Pediatrician in their practice on the show would be a career game changer in both industries. I happened to have had lunch with just about everyone, and they all are leaning towards you. These Hollywood streets are talking, and they are saying that there simply is no stronger candidate than the notable, Dr. Kristina Rosario."

"Like you said, this is Hollywood. A fake doctor, with fake boobs, and a fake accent might come along and stomp on my dreams. Londy, I think that I may give them about 2 more weeks, then I am going to start diversifying my dreams."

"Come on T... Don't make any drastic decisions out of emotions of uncertainty. Why don't you take some time off. Before you say no, and yes, I realize that you just drove down to spend Thanksgiving with your parents, but an overnight stay can't be what the good doctor orders for the holidays. Drive back down to Fontana and soak up some of the holiday preparations. Your parents will be overjoyed and you always come back with that seasonal glow about you that 24 hours just don't quite do. Besides, the 30-day countdown to Christmas and 29 days until your birthday has begun. But who's counting?"

"Well, just like I informed my parents, I don't plan on

making a big deal out of either Christmas or my birthday this year.   The holiday may just end up being a neglected dried-up poinsettia in the corner of my condo and reheated take-out on the agenda.   Actually, I'm considering volunteering to cover a shift at the hospital for someone who is not busily chasing hopes and dreams and have their life all planned out. Perhaps a struggling physician who is being chased by their dreams and juggling quality time with a spouse, kids, fur babies, a private practice…"

"Absolutely not! Don't even think about it. I promise you that we will have much to celebrate," London concluded firmly.

"I have to run. Someone is at my door. It's probably my poke bowl and bubble tea. The cranberry flavor is only available for the rest of the month. I will call you back later."

"Enjoy Tina. Talk soon."

Kristina ended her call with London and headed out of her apartment and down 7 floors to the lobby. Exiting the stairwell, she stepped into the corridor where she could see a portion of the brightly lit lobby. The slate-colored carpet led to the light gray marble floor with wide charcoal veins that complimented the floor to ceiling glass wall that revealed the picturesque artistic view of the row of cobalt blue accent planters and palm tree trunks in front of Gracie's Greek Restaurant, across the street. Kristina loved both the day and night view of Gracie's. The lights all year around cast a welcoming glow during a night stroll. It was one of the reasons she purchased her unit. She repeatedly would say that the view of Gracie's lights never gets old.

As Kristina turned the corner to enter the lobby, she noticed three women decorating a large Christmas tree in the middle of the reception area. It had to be at least 9 feet tall, she thought.

It was certainly larger than last year's tree, which was grand and beautifully decorated. Kristina paused for a moment and looked on while one of the ladies climbed halfway up a ladder hanging red ribbons trimmed in gold along the way. The giant ornaments of green, white, and red reminded her of home and how her mother incorporates Mexican American heritage in her over the top holiday decorations. She thought that maybe her friend London may be right about driving back down to Fontana for a few days. She decided that she would give it some more thought. She planned to decide before the day was over. But for the moment, she was hungry, and prioritized matters over mind.

"Hey there Jasper. Do you have something for me?" Kristina asked the tall well-dressed bearded gentleman.

"Yes, Dr. Rosario. Your lunch was just delivered. I could have brought it up to you," he said with insistence. "In fact, I was just about to…"

"Oh no Jasper, I really needed to stretch my legs a bit. So much so that I actually took the stairs," she replied humorously.

"Oh, before I forget Doc, you have another package, well an envelope that I signed for this morning. Let me get it."

Jasper returned quickly, then handed her a bag of food, a drink, and the envelope stored in a locked drawer behind the concierge counter.

"May I trouble you for a small request Dr. Rosario?"

"Certainly, Jasper of course. What can I do for you?"

"I was hoping that you could sign my copy of your latest

book. I picked it up as an early Christmas present for my wife. She is quite the fan I must say. Since she has been on bed rest, she reads all the shameless tabloid as a guilty pleasure. She even says that we may be seeing you on that reality show..um.. Celebrity Doctors: Practicing Hollywood."

"Well Jasper, you know that only half of what is said in those rags have merit... but as long as they spelled Kristina with a K and not a C, then I won't be mad at that rumor," she winked. "And yes, yes, yes, I would love to autograph a copy for Nadine as I am a big fan of hers as well and her chocolate gingerbread cookie recipe. My staff still thinks that I should be marketing the batch that they think I baked for last year's Christmas party. You know after the baby, if she decides to market her cookies or open that bakery, she will have a customer for life in me."

After signing Jasper's copy of her book, Kristina stared at the name of the law firm's return address that seemed to have an uncertain familiarity with it. She gave a little melancholy chuckle reading aloud the law firm named Jolly Law, located in Jolly, California printed on the eco-friendly envelope. Instinctively she thought that this letter would have otherwise been mistaken for junk mail had there not been a requested signature-upon-receipt notice affixed. She took the elevator back up to her apartment, never taking her eyes off the envelope. Before the stainless-steel elevator doors opened, she ripped the seal and pulled out 2 pages of typewritten correspondence with the words; *FINAL NOTICE* stamped at the top of the page.

Dear Ms. Rosario, Beneficiary
Our firm has been designated to inform and assist you regarding the

distribution of assets of Pamelia Zavala who passed away November 7, 2023. The estate has been held in trust pending your notification and response.

As executor of Ms. Zavala's estate, we hereby notify you that you have been named the sole beneficiary to the inheritance of real estate property, Jolly, California to include the following assets, but not limited to:

1 Ski Lodge, 1 youth camp, 1 clinic, 1 schoolhouse, 1 bakery, 1 candy shop, 1 toy store, 1 restaurant, 1 multiplex event center, 1 post office, barber/hair salon, 2 animal stables, 2 barns, gas station, fire station, estate of living quarters, and the beneficiary account that manages assets.

The inheritance of real estate property of Jolly, California to include the following liabilities, but not limited to:

Salaries of staff, official duties, council members appointments. To claim or disclaim must be made in person before the city council 7 days after the official reading of the last Will and Testament of Pamelia Zavala on December 17, 2025, at 3:30pm, after which time the court will be petitioned for guidance to distribute your inheritance properly.

Transportation arrangements have been made and can be retrieved at any time before December 1, 2025, at the Los Angeles County Clerk's office for city offices.

Should you have any questions, feel free to contact us at 1-800-555-6559

Or visit our website www.cityofjolly.org

CHAPTER TWO

THE WILL AND THE WAY

A far cry from its hay day, but still unique in its own right, sits in mourning the small township of Jolly, California, elevation 8,000 feet; population 364.

With the 25th month approaching of being left on their own unmotivated accord, fueled by sorrow and despair, the citizens of Jolly now recognize the importance of selecting new leadership, if not for anything else but to restore a sense of normalcy and a glimmer of hope for a joyful tomorrow.

The loss of Pamelia Zavala, endearingly known as Peazy, was felt by everyone in this small close-knit community. She was the heart of Jolly for more than the 69 years of oath of duty. Her love and sincerity was systemically felt by every person and animal that calls Jolly home. At the age of 94, she was as vibrant as anyone half her age. She took ill right before the trip to formally initiate the induction of her successor, whom she watched in secret for 25 years.

Peazy routinely put everyone's needs before her own. Only a discreet few knew that she unselfishly allowed her heir time to fulfill their personal goals and dreams rather than burden them with the option of assuming the responsibility of a task that they had no clue even existed. It was said that Peazy had the ability to hear the wishes in the wind of the next in line and that she often granted it unconditionally; even if it meant that she would extend her ascendancy beyond a normal term that would have otherwise allowed her to convalesce and retire more gracefully.

The overall consensus of today's Town Hall Meeting was extremely positive, yet a hint of skepticism did not escape Marvin Lee's face as he did not share the sentimental optimism that his neighbors placed in their potential new benefactor. In fact, Marvin Lee Mass Jr. preferred spending quality time with animals over human beings on any given day. Jolly's handsome resident veterinarian would love to see his beloved hometown rekindle and flourish. He thought that more days of disappointment were on the horizon if Jollians put all of their faith in some big city outsider. Marvin Lee also loved Peazy and probably missed her more than anyone else. As much as he would be happy to retreat to the ranch, he knew that Peazy would want him to do anything and everything within his power to make Kristina feel welcomed.

◆ ◆ ◆

Traveling through the mountainous region was indeed beautiful. The route was scenic and less windy than expected for this time of year. The ascend to higher elevation and deep into the mountain range, the snow-capped mountain peaks appear welcoming. The small towns along the way were a pleasant change from miles of rocky terrain. The authority check points for tire safety inspections was a reminder that they were quite a long way from the city.

"London thanks again for coming with me on such short notice. This is just the craziest thing I've ever heard of," Kristina said, still feeling confused and curious.

"Tina, it is the craziest thing I have heard of too. And believe me, in this business, not to mention being a black girl growing up in Compton, I have heard and seen crazy. Besides, even though I can only stay for one day, there is no way in the world I would let you go anywhere alone under these strange circumstances," London replied in her eccentric but consoling manner. "I'm kind of happy just to see you take a break from your routine," she added.

"Alrighty now not you too. The staff at the hospital basically kicked me out the door, claiming that I do not take time to smell the roses. I doubt if there are any roses up here in these mountains."

"That and apparently a signal," London replies while checking her phone.

"Lon, in all honesty, I don't know whether to be excited or afraid. You know, I haven't been up to the ski mountains since the college study trip in Big Bear where we got no studying done, Kristina recanted with one squinted and one widened eye.

"Ya know, I think I remember going and then coming home. Everything in between is still a blur," London countered.

"Some things should stay a blur, just for deniability, if you know what I mean." They both laughed, then gave each other a high-five hand clap and a synchronized finger snap.

"Speaking of which, Kristina," London's tone changed to more serious in nature. "I have known you since college and we shared being adopted in common. I have met your parents, and they are just the best mother and father that any adult or child could have wished for. And the Christmas celebrations! Oh, my goodness! I loved going home with you during the holidays. I am still impressed by the decorations outside as well as inside. The artificial snow was top tier girlfriend."

"Can you believe that my parents didn't even celebrate Christmas until we became a family?"

"No way!" London replied shockingly.

"Yes way. They said that I brought the joy of Christmas and the magic of the season into their lives."

"So now, this Pamelia person, were your parents able to shed any light on how she is connected to you? Especially with literally leaving you such a substantial estate."

"No, they did not have any idea. They just said that the circumstances around my adoption were somewhat unorthodox. They didn't go into details but said that we should talk about it more in person. Because of the urgency to meet the deadline expressed in the letter, we had to postpone that talk for when I return. My parents made it a point to express that they loved me so much and that they were forever grateful and welcomed any opportunity for my birth family to share in the gift of love that they were blessed with."

"Your parents are such amazing people. They raised an amazing daughter too."

"Thanks, Londy. Their daughter has an amazing best friend." They smiled at each other.

"Driver, my apologies. I mean Brian, how much further

away is Jolly?" London inquired. We have been riding for almost 3 hours.

"About 15 more minutes ma'am."

"Thank you."

"I haven't been able to get a phone signal for the last ten minutes. I sure hope that they have Wi-Fi in town. I have a meeting with the network this week, but first I really need to see what this law firm is talking about by implying that there is a level of responsibility that is attached to this inheritance. I just hope that there are no conflicts, because once the show executives make their decision, things are going to move pretty fast with contract negotiations, disclosures, NDAs, shoot schedule, etc. etc."

"Do you know that I have not had a moment to think about Practicing Hollywood since I got this letter from the law firm in Jolly?"

"Ladies, we are here," announced the driver.

They looked out of the rear driver-side passenger window and read the town sign:

Welcome To Jolly California
"Santa's Rest Stop"
Population 364
Land gifted by the Serrano

As they rode a mile into the city limits and down through Main Street, which consisted of 3 blocks of wall-adjacent storefront businesses on both sides of the street, they immediately noticed the Mayberry-at-Christmas vintage vibe.

The roundabouts at each end of Main Street had an enormous Pine tree. Both trees appeared to be in the process of being decorated for the Holidays. Kristina thought it all to be unusually late in the season, especially for a town named Jolly, where Santa apparently makes a stop. She compared the fact that the malls and shopping centers in the Los Angeles area begin to look a lot like Christmas long before Thanksgiving; some even, the day after Halloween. Kristina thought to herself that her parents would have had Main Street of Jolly, California decked with Silver Bells, Bows and Holly from end to end just as they do on their cul-de-sac starting November 27th through New Years Day.

After pulling into the half-circular driveway of a quaint little apple green Victorian-style bed and breakfast, Kristina and London stood beside the car looking over at *The Jolly Inn* sign that had an upside down candy cane as the J in Jolly while their driver, Brian collected their designer luggage from the trunk.

"Hmm, I guess this is Jolly," Kristina sighed.

"It is certainly not the Hollywood glitz that you are used to, but we humbly call this place home," interjected a tenor-toned male voice that startled the ladies.

The two friends turned around quickly to find out that the face of the unexpected voice belonged to an attractive, clean shaved bronze-skinned, native American man with long black hair pulled back behind his ears. His plaid shirt and denim jacket did not camouflage his muscular physique. His chestnut brown eyes were dreamy and could almost distract one from the undeniable look of contempt that the rest of his face displayed.

"Oh sir, I promise you, no offense was intended," Kristina attempted to recover. "I was just thinking about the name..."

"Don't bother with the explanation. Let me get your bags and get you checked into your more than likely less than delightful accommodations."

Kristina and London looked at each other as if they were caught with their hands in the cookie jar, again. They both also noticed that their unkind greeter's jeans were certainly serving up rugged couture. With both hands full, he carried all of their baggage in one trip. They made haste and followed him up the potted poinsettia lined stairs to the wrap around porch and then through the front door.

The charm and coziness immediately greeted all senses from the smell of freshly baked sugar cookies to the warmth of the crackling wood burning in the fireplace.

The welcoming smile from the balding round belly Innkeeper was particularly comforting after such a long ride and awkward first contact interaction with a local.

"Good afternoon, Dr. Rosario and Ms. Haney. My name is Bishop. Welcome to Jolly and welcome to The Jolly Inn. You will be in rooms 8 and 9. Marvin Lee is taking care of your luggage, and my wife is preparing a light lunch for you."

"Thank you kindly, Mr. Bishop. I'm sure that everything will be fine. I know that I did not give a good first impression to the bellman who has our luggage."

"Bellman?" Laughed Bishop. "You mean Marvin Lee? I assure you, he's harmless, a softy even, beneath his rough exterior. Don't tell him that I told you, but he would literally give you the shirt off his back."

"Girl, I would be more than happy to test that theory out if I were you," London nudged and whispered facetiously.

Marvin came downstairs with his hands resting in his front pockets and joined the three who were in conversation at the reception area.

"Hey Bishop, I put your guest's luggage upstairs. Do you need anything else before I take off?" Marvin asked without making eye contact with the ladies.

"Hello. Marvin Lee?" Kristina waved lightly to get his attention; although standing less that 2 feet away from him, yet feeling invisible. "I was hoping that we could get a do over. Hi I'm Kristina," she said smiling and extended her hand for a handshake.

"Yes, I know who you are, Dr. Rosario." With hesitation, he reluctantly shook her hand that appeared to be suspended in mid-air awaiting his response. There was an undeniable cosmic trance that occurred when they made physical contact, followed by a noticeable delay in the separation and retreat of their hands.

The presence of Mrs. Bishop standing next to them holding a

tray with the 2 remaining cups of hot cocoa and a plate of cookies broke their concentration. In their peripheral view stood a short brunette woman wearing a candy cane print apron over a red turtleneck sweater dress and a cheerful grin on her face.

"Oh, thank you Mrs. Bishop. This is lovely," Kristina said as she grabbed a cup and a cookie from the tray.

"Call me Zula, Dr. Rosario,"

"Okay Zula, but only if you call me Kristina."

"Agreed. Welcome to Jolly. I really hope that you will enjoy your stay here with us."

"I'm sure I will, Zula.Thank you for hosting us. "

"I hate to interrupt a good time, but you young ladies may want to take a moment to settle in. Your driver, Brian will be here at 2:30 to take you over to meet with Randall at the law office for the reading of the Will," announced Bishop.

"So, you know about that?" asked London

"Sure. The entire town knows. There are no secrets about important events in Jolly. Peazy's Will reading is indeed an important event," Bishop replied.

"Who is Peazy?" asked Kristina

"Pamelia Zavala," answered Marvin Lee.

"You know, it was Marvin Lee who started calling her

Peazy when he was 2 years old and it stuck," Bishop said with a chuckle.

"I bet he was so cute, " she replied with smile.

"Still is," mumbled London

"Okay. I have to get back to the ranch," interrupted Marvin Lee to change the subject and make a polite and quick exit. "There was a colt born this morning and I want to check in on mom and baby."

CHAPTER THREE

THE EIGHTH WONDER

T he freshly shoveled walkway leading to the entry door of Jolly Law on Main was interpreted as inviting and expected. Randall West, Esquire Attorney at law, was engraved on the door with an emblem etching of a scale with a gold inlay. What was unexpected was the lack of professional stuffiness that is usually associated with law offices once inside. Instead of the dark wood tones associated with legal desperation and disparity, it was wall-to-wall winter white with a gallery of art on the wall of snowscape and nature's winter woodland beauty in this small office.

Tori, paralegal and receptionist, greeted Kristina and London with excitement and giddiness of a 19-year-old Jollonian meeting a celebrity. She used every ounce of inner strength and containment to keep her promise to her mentor and employer to save all questions about Hollywood, Beverly Hills, fashion, etc. until after the reading of the Will.

Tori offered the ladies a choice of coffee, tea, bottled water, hot cocoa, or apple cider while they waited for Mr. West to finish up on a call. She expounded upon their interest in the wall art and proudly shared that Randall West is also a novice photographer and what hung on the walls were his actual pieces. Both women were extremely impressed with what they were seeing. Even more-so was London, when the tall dark and handsome man exited the closed office door.

"Sweet baby Jesus, I think I will have that large hot cocoa after all," London sighed.

"Coming right up! Would you like marshmallows with it?" Tori asked, but did not get a response. Kristina nudged London with her elbow after Tori repeated the question about marshmallows.

"Huh? Um, yes. Marshmallows will be fine," she recovered, but kept her eyes glued on the attorney artist who to her looked like a work of art himself.

"Hello ladies. I apologize that I was not here to greet you. I'm Randall West. I hope that Tori took good care of you in my absence. Nice to finally meet you Dr. Rosario and Ms. Haney," he added as he extended a handshake to each of them.

"Kristina, please."

"Kristina," he repeats with a nod and a smile.

"Ms...Mrs. Haney?"

"London."

"London, my pleasure," he replied holding her hand and looking into her eyes.

"The pleasure is mine indeed, Randall. So, Tori tells us that this is some of your work. These pieces are exceptional and exquisite. Here is my card. I'd love to see more."

"Oh, you are an attorney as well?" Randall asked, after reading her card.

"I am an entertainment attorney. Contract law and representing an exclusive clientele; including 2-time best-selling author, celebrity pediatrician, and reality TV star, Dr. Kristina Rosario...and perhaps Randall West, Esquire, photography artist some day?"

"I don't think that my amateur photos qualify me or your level of representation," he laughed. "Please step into my office. Tori will bring your beverages."

Randall West's office seemed more in line with the office of a lawyer. There were wall-to-wall law books on mahogany bookshelves and a matching desk with a black high-back leather chair. The conference table, however, was more rustic yet artistic and crafty. It was made of a mix of white birch, oak, and holly. The view of the snow-capped mountain from the window was an interior and exterior example of nature's art and the art of bringing the outside inside. One could almost expect to see God's signature in the lower right-hand corner of the window.

"We are here for the official reading of the Last Will and Testament of Pamelia E. Zavala. As stipulated, there will be a video portion of the testament that is primarily confidential and intended only for the beneficiary. Let the record show that that all parties present and are in agreement with the terms of the reading."

As the list of properties, accounts, and duties associated with said properties and said accounts were read, Kristina began to feel overwhelmed. This was a level of anxiety that she was not used to experiencing. She had more questions than answers and could not continue with the reading. She requested a moment to take a break and assess some of what she heard.

Randall thought that it would be an appropriate time to play the video in hopes that Kristina would receive the clarity that she desperately desired. He stepped out of the room to signal Tori, who quickly brought in a fresh cup of cocoa and a star-shaped sugar cookie on a plate. She sat them in front of Kristina and left. Randall handed her a remote control and left the office behind Tori.

Kristina sat holding the remote control tightly in her hand and stared at the dark monitor for a few minutes after hearing the door close, until her mind matched the external silence that engulfed her.

Not really recognizing the exact moment when her auto reflex kicked in, the face of an elderly woman with wavy silver hair and kind, yet tired eyes appeared on the screen. Kristina was unable at the time to discern if the sense of familiarity for a split second was just a matter of wishful thinking or subliminal self-delusion.

"Hello Kristina. If you are seeing this my dear, it means that I did not get to have a final conversation with you before my transition about just how special you are to me and to the citizens of Jolly."

"Final?" muttered Kristina.

"I know what you are thinking and yes, final. Please take a bite of the cookie before you and things will become clear," instructed Pamelia.

Taking in a full deep breath, Kristina conceded and complied. She wanted more answers. She exhaled then took a bite of the star-shaped sugar cookie on the dessert plate before her. Within seconds, an indistinct blurred image of clouds followed by a glow of an amber bright light occurred right before a series of life events flashed before her mind's eyes. Kristina closed her eyes tightly while she saw visions of herself as a child in school walking past Pamelia in the hallway. She recalled feeling a happy sensation after passing her and remembering that she was really sad moments before seeing this kind faced lady walk by. Next Kristina saw herself graduating from high school and seeing Pamelia in the audience and locking eyes with her as she delivered her valedictorian speech.

Kristina's respirations increased as sadness suddenly fell upon her when she remembered the loss of a newborn baby that was delivered during her first year of medical school. Her eyes began to swell with tears before a calming sensation was felt. Kristina saw the anonymous doctor who consoled her that night in the vision. She remembered that it was this doctor that gave her the strength to continue and to be able to comfort the family who was devastated. She recalled later looking to thank the kind physician who came to her aid but was not able to find her or anyone who recognized her as being a part of the rotation on duty. Unsure, Kristina felt that she may have even interacted with Pamelia occasionally in her dreams.

As the cinema in her mind began to fade to black, the view of the video monitor came into focus with the Pamelia's face paused. Kristina experienced a sensation of warmth, similar to a hug. Kristina felt relaxed and safe. Then on cue, the audio resumed.

"Anticipating all of the questions that you may have my dearest is probably where I will fall short, as for many of the answers that you seek, only time and experience will reveal. First things first. Yes, you and I are are family. Not by blood in the traditional science way, but by Essence. Now beloved, explaining Essence is a bit more intricate.

Essence is a magical substance of goodness sprinkled throughout the world. Individuals infused with Essence are connected in the same manner as a network of genetics. I was an Essence baby, and so were you. In fact, the world is full of Essence, thankfully.

Now there are places that are as special as we are. Places like Jolly and the North Pole; places that are the 8th wonders of the world per say, if they could say that is. Unfortunately, places like Jolly require a dedication of heart and commitment by a person of Essence to oversee its ability to thrive, sustain, and advance. I am afraid that Jolly is in need of more Essence than I had left in me to take them into the next century. Jolly needs you Kristina, and you need Jolly more than you probably know.

Lastly Kristina, and most importantly, you have only 7 days to decide. After 7 days, your memory of any of this and the reality behind the true existence of Jolly, California will vanish. If you decide to stay, you must take a second bite of the sugar cookie to fulfil your destiny as the new Essence of Jolly. I want you to know that whether you decide to share your life with the people of Los Angeles or the people of Jolly, it has been the honor of my earthly lifetime to spend the last part of my journey proudly watching you become the exceptional caregiver that you are.

I have charged both Randall and Marvin Lee with assisting you with anything that you may need during your stay. I trust them to take care of you. As it was said to me, I now pass to you; May our Essence connect and may your Essence flourish."

CHAPTER FOUR

THE JOLLY TOUR GUIDE

As Kristina continued to stare out of the window of her cozy room where she watched the sunset and darkening of the room, then of the sunrise that shed light in the room and onto another day. From the oversized stuffed chair positioned beside her queen-sized bed with six large pillows and a matching floral and plaid duvet that was not slept in last night, she was perched as she replayed the events of yesterday's Will reading in her head repeatedly.

Kristina did not unpack her suitcase because she was contemplating leaving the mountain with London and leaving behind all that she was unable to process. She felt that she could not begin to unpack all that she was told that could lie ahead should she decide to stick around. Kristina wished for a moment that she had a double shift at the hospital to pull just so that she could focus her attention elsewhere. She was shocked that she managed to fall asleep as she rarely slept long on any given day. Although the soft knock at the door broke her concentration, Kristina remained silent. She looked at her attire and realized that she was still wearing her clothing from the day before. She thought that she should at least shower before the long drive home. She heard the sound of shuffling paper then noticed that there appeared to be a note that was slid under the closed door.

She walked over to the door, picked it up, and read it.

Hey Tina,

I had a breakfast date with Randall before heading back to LA for an important meeting that I could not reschedule. He offered me a ride home and I accepted.

I missed you at dinner last night. I didn't want to wake you. I hope that you rested well.

It may not be a bad idea to spend a few more days off the grid smelling roses.

Call me when you get back.

XOXO London

Kristina smiled. She was happy to see her friend, London, go on a date, especially since it was an activity that neither of them had done in quite a while. She thought that for that reason alone, the trip to Jolly was not a complete waste. She didn't look forward to the long ride back alone to the city. She folded the note and placed it on the bed and headed to the shower.

"There are no roses to smell in a village of snow," she said aloud before entering the gentle and steamy dispersed flow of water.

◆ ◆ ◆

As Kristina descended the stairs of the bed and breakfast, the aroma of breakfast danced in her head. She inhaled deeply to fill her lungs and savored the delightful air that she could almost taste. The Bishops greeted her with their usual cheer and directed her to the kitchen where a breakfast buffet had been prepared for the guests of the Inn.

Kristina was quite surprised to see Marvin Lee sitting at the table eating pancakes and making conversation with a couple finishing up their breakfast. Surprisingly to Kristina, when he looked up and saw her, she saw that he had a softer look in his eyes then, than when they first met. In fact, she thought she saw a quick smile. She grabbed a coffee cup and poured a hot cup of coffee and joined him at the table. She smiled at the couple leaving the table passing.

"Good morning, Marvin Lee."

"Good morning Doct...good morning, Kristina," he corrected and smiled. She smiled back. "You really should try the pancakes. They are the best in Jolly, I must say."

"I'm sure they are if you endorse them, but coffee is usually my breakfast. Now rumor has it that I am a big lunch kind of girl," she said with a touch of humor.

"Well, I happen to know that Jolly has a coffee shop that can actually compete with those big city blends, if you are game to find out."

"You know what Marvin Lee, I think I will take you up on that."

"Great. Grab your jacket and gloves and I will meet you on the porch in 10 minutes. I am going to just grab another small stack of pancakes. I wouldn't want to hurt Zula's feelings if she comes back to a half platter of leftover pancakes."

"Well eat up, because we wouldn't want to hurt Zula's feelings now, would we?" Kristina joked and laughed before heading upstairs to grab her coat.

Surprisingly, Main Street appeared to be more festive today through Kristina's eyes. Marvin Lee turned out to be more than a gracious tour guide. He pointed out several businesses along the way that they passed by on their walk in the brisk morning air. The smell of roasting chestnuts and freshly baked pastries surrounded them like a soft breeze of pleasantness.

Just a block away from The Jolly Inn was *RUTH CRINGLE'S CAFE*. The top sellers on the menu were of course the popular hot cider and hot cocoa. Marvin Lee ordered the Peppermint Latte for himself and ordered the Jolly Java Jubilee for Kristina. The smile and the eye-roll reflex after she sipped the Triple-J confirmed that their little mountain town's coffee could hold its own against the big city gourmet coffee shops.

"Oh, my goodness, this is amazing! Is this cranberry infused whipped cream? Cranberry is my favorite fruit."

"It sure is. And what a coincidence that cranberries are also my favorite fruit. Cranberries are high in vitamin C, E, K, Manganese, and antioxidants."

"Wow, I am impressed."

"Maybe tomorrow, we can visit the Sugar Plum Bakery, where they make the best cranberry muffins, cranberry loaf, cranberry cookies, cranberry bread..."

"Okay, okay, I saw that movie, but I think that it was shrimp everything."

"Hey, I saw that one too. Now I have the urge to take off running down Main Street." Marvin Lee and Kristina laughed intensely, until their eyes met, causing them to yield to a shared unspoken and obvious attraction.

Kristina force released her gaze and pointed across the street to the sign trio that caught her eye just moments before he did.

The Jolly People Clinic

The Jolly Pet Clinic

The Jolly Toy Clinic

"Would you mind if we checked that out?" Kristina asked, sounding genuinely intrigued.

"Now that, Dr. Rosario, is or shall I say was what we called Jolly's Infirmary Row. It used to be very active at one time, but as the calipers of modern toys desired by children changed to more electronic types, the need for the toy clinic was cancelled along with the nostalgia of fixing the arm of a doll or new tire on a truck. Then we had the doggie in the window that was popular with the tourists who were gifting puppies for Christmas. Many of the guests who brought their fur family members along on vacation really loved the doggie spa experience."

"Oh, that sounds adorable."

"Yes. Dad had lots of adorable ideas," Marvin Lee mumbled.

"Oh, that's right, your father is the town veterinarian. And what about the People Clinic?"

"So, Old Doc Johnson is semi-retired and other than the basic house calls, folks go over to Big Bear for anything more serious in nature. And then there was Peazy. She used to be the Midwife back in the day."

"Midwife? Really?"

"Yes. She even had plans to open a midwifery school."

"So, what happened?"

"Who knows. She tried to be everything for everyone and her dreams pretty much...I don't know," he conceded. "I better walk you back to the Inn. I have to get back out to the ranch, but I will be by a little later. I have instructions to take you over to Mistletoe Manor."

"Mistletoe Manor? What's that?"

"Mistletoe Manor is the most important place in Jolly. It's the house of Essence. It is...it was where Peazy lived," he said with sadness.

"Um, I don't know about that. I am not even sure if I will be here later," Kristina replied while trying to think of an excuse to hide her deep rooted concern and and uneasiness. She did not feel that she could share a fear with a stranger that she hadn't admitted to herself since the reading of the Will.

"No?"

"Yeah, um. Its just that I might be going back to LA with my friend this afternoon," she said slowly with her head hung.

"You mean the friend that left with Randall this morning?"

"So you know about that, huh? Of course you do. I forgot that nothing happens in Jolly that everyone isn't aware of."

"You know, I pretty much expected that you would. I guess you can't take the girl out of the city or the city out of the girl," Marvin Lee blurted sarcastically, then sped up his pace leaving Kristina behind.

"Hey wait up, Marvin Lee! All of this is a bit much. I mean this, whatever this is... its just not exactly what I thought it would be."

"Well, you are exactly what I thought you would be."

"What do you mean by that?" Kristina shouted and stopped her chase. Her heavy breathing began to slow back to a normal rate.

"What I mean, Dr. Rosario, is that Peazy wasted her time and her faith in you. Heck, Essence was wasted on you," he said slowly and deliberately while stopping in his tracks to face her to land his words.

Kristina stood still, paralyzed from the blow of his words. She watched Marvin Lee walk past the Inn and climb into the driver's side of a bright red pick-up truck.

As the truck sped past her, she noticed a painted sign on the door that read: Reindeer Ranch Youth Program.

CHAPTER FIVE

MISTRESS OF MISTLETOE MANOR

Groggily, Kristina lifted her head from the bed of soft pillows. She realized that not only had she fallen asleep, but also from the orange hues and muted colors on the horizon, her slumber had lasted for hours. She rubbed her stomach after a giant stretch and yawn because hunger was becoming more pronounced by the minute.

Kristina walked past the room that London once occupied. She placed her hand on the door and wished that she had her friend to confide in about how torn she was feeling inside. She decided against calling her so that at least one of them could be able to enjoy the Jolly experience. As Kristina's mind started to drift, she became startled when Mr. Bishop came around the corner of the hallway.

"Hello there Kristina. I thought I heard you stirring about. Zula checked on you earlier today around lunchtime. London mentioned before leaving for the city that you don't usually sleep well."

"It looks like I have been getting plenty of sleep since I have been here."

"My buddy Brian left a message about an hour ago that since it was getting late, he would just wait for a call in the morning should you be in need of his services. Oh, before I forget Kristina, Zula left you a plate in the kitchen, just in case you woke up with an appetite. I hope you like turkey salad on wheat."

"Sounds wonderful Bishop. And yes, I am famished," she smiled.

"Then I will escort you down to the kitchen, my lady," Bishop extended his bended arm, and she curtsied and took hold. "Oh, before I forget, Randall West sent over a package for you from his law office. It is near the front door."

"Thanks. Hey Bishop, what can you tell me about Mistletoe Manor?"

"Well, what would you like to know?"

"I'm not really sure. Marvin Lee said that I was supposed to go there today, but we had a disagreement of sorts. All I know is that Pamelia Zavala lived there."

"Yes, she did. She was the most amazing human being. I feel her absence every day. But for some reason, I have felt a similar sense of completeness since you arrived," he said drifting in thought of Peazy as he spoke. "But Mistletoe Manor is nearby. If you really want to go, I will be happy to take you over when you finish your sandwich."

"If it isn't a bother, I'd like that. Maybe there is a key in the package the attorney sent over today."

"Maybe, but if Mistletoe is your destiny, you wouldn't need a key anyway," he chuckled.

Kristina looked perplexed by his statement, but her thoughts quickly moved on to the sandwich splendidly presented before her on a glossy white salad plate. The tall glass of milk reminded Kristina of her childhood, but it was seeing the crust removed from the bread that took her moment of nostalgia to the next level. She almost wished that she had time to enjoy the moment, her thoughts were now of the anticipation of the adventure of visiting Pamelia's home that made two bites of the sandwich and a swig of milk suffice before racing out to Bishop's truck.

◆ ◆ ◆

Mistletoe Manor was simply breathtaking from first sight. Kristina was caught up in a plethora of emotional gymnastics. The whimsical Christmas decorations generated an authenticity of holiday enchantment unlike anything she had ever seen. She felt the awakening of child-like innocence that adulthood smothers until unrecognizable or evaporates.

Kristina exited Bishop's truck with only smiles exchanged, great big smiles. She looked up into the night sky as light snow flurries began to fall. She opened her mouth and stuck her tongue out so that a few flakes would land on her tongue as she instantly recalled a forgotten family trip to the mountains. She remembered feeling as if she was inside of a snow globe. It was the same feeling that she felt at that very moment.

Kristina found the lighting of the pathway with each step she took towards the front door to be extremely inviting. She pressed the doorbell and sighed when she heard the melody of Carol of the Bells chiming. It was indeed her favorite Christmas Carol.

A split moment of disappointment shadowed her face when there was no answer. She looked back at Bishop who was still sitting idle in his truck in the manor's circular driveway with the interior light on. As she conceded that the possibility of a visit was not going to happen tonight, she caught a glimpse of Bishop smiling in the distance before he drove off leaving her on the porch of Mistletoe Manor. She realized that her wave in his rear-view mirror meant that she would have to walk back to the Inn.

The falling snowflakes had begun to fall heavier, and the gusting winds were rapidly building up. Kristina was suddenly reminded of what Bishop had said to her. "If you belonged there, you wouldn't need a key." Oddly enough, she gave in to not rationalizing. On a whim Kristina grabbed the doorknob. Her eyes widened as she saw that the brass knob glowed before her with the touch of her hand. The door became ajar with no physical effort at all. She could see as the door continued to slowly open on its own, that the inside of Mistletoe Manor, the interior Christmas decorations were as mystically beautiful as the exterior. Kristina mumbled to herself, "Here we go Alice," then stepped all in without reservation.

All of her senses tingled as she took in the view of several lit Christmas trees of various sizes all around her in this grand foyer she had just entered.

Kristina didn't know which direction to begin her self-guided tour. A small glow appeared on the large marble-top table with a dark wood base. Lying next to an extremely large-scaled poinsettia flower arrangement was a red envelope with her name written in glitter. The note written on the snow-white paper read:

Greetings Kristina,

Welcome to Mistletoe Manor. Make yourself at home.
Everything that you will need is available or can be obtained. The
house staff here may not be openly evident, but each wall has a call
button and an intercom system for your use.

Explore your new home and unlock the answers that you desire.
Connect with the essence that links your past, present and future.

Best wishes,
Pamelia

Kristina didn't quite know how to process what she just read. Surprisingly, her cellphone vibrated instead of ringing. Her concentration was broken. She was pleasantly surprised to receive a telephone call, as the Wi-Fi service was spotty at the Inn. She quickly reached in her pocket to retrieve her phone and answer the call. She didn't even check to see who it was. She was glad to connect with anyone outside of Jolly at that moment.

"Hello. This is Dr. Rosario."

"Why so formal Tina?"

"Oh, London, I didn't realize it was you. I must have turned off my ringer by mistake or something."

"Well don't be so excited. I'm just checking on you. You were like passed out when I left."

"Sorry Londy girl. I must have been more exhausted than I thought. Anyway, how was your breakfast with the handsome Jolly lawyer?"

"Let's say that lunch, dinner, and a night cap that followed was my dream date. He reminds me of a younger version of Denzel Washington or Barack Obama. Who knew we did snow mountains? Anyway, I didn't want to leave, but I couldn't reschedule meetings."

"Speaking of meetings, London, any news about the show?"

"About that. I have good and not so good news. Good news, they are still interested in casting you."

"And...the not so good?"

"They now have one other candidate in the running."

"Aw London," she sighed in disappointment.

"But only one other candidate Tina and I am sure that you are the best choice. Trust me and let me work my magic."

"Speaking of magic, you would never guess where I am right now."

"Hopefully at the Jolly Inn where I left you," London replied matter of factly.

"Jolly yes, but not at the Inn. I am basically a few blocks

away at this amazing estate called, Mistletoe Manor."

"Are you alone?"

"I don't think so."

"Ok there is something creepy about that answer.

"Yeah, well I just read a letter that I think was from Pamelia Zavala saying that this place is practically mine and that there was house staff discretely here, or something like that."

"What else did it say? Read it to me."

"I will pass on the reread right now. It sounded like some Christmas Carol Scrooge stuff, and I am not the one."

"Why don't you just go back to the Inn since you aren't far."

"Well, it's snowing and it's really beautiful here. You know I don't sleep much at night so exploring sounds interesting. First thing I am going to do is meet the house-staff."

"Ok Tina, that sounds like a good idea. Just keep your phone charged and close by and call me if you need to. I will check on you in the morning."

"Good night bestie."

"Niters bestie."

Kristina ended her call and went directly to the wall of the first adjoining room off of the foyer that appeared to be a living or sitting room. She pressed a call button once. She said hello a few times since she was unsure how it worked. She was startled when she heard a woman's voice present in the room instead of through the speaker as she had expected.

"Yes, Ms. Kristina. May I be of assistance," asked the tall and thin freckled-face young woman wearing a crisp white blouse and black pencil skirt. Her face was kind.

"Oh wow, you scared me," huffed Kristina as she held her hand against her chest.

"I apologize. I'm so sorry..." she replied sincerely.

"Oh no don't be. Let's just start over. I'm Kristina Rosario, but apparently you know that," she chuckled to relax the woman's face. "And you are?

"My name is Marie, ma'am. I am the west wing manager. I am so happy to finally meet you. May I get you anything to eat, drink, or would you like me to take you to your quarters?"

"You mean I have quarters, Marie?"

Marie giggled and covered her mouth to hide her less than formal disposition. Kristina laughed and welcomed the more casual encounter. She felt more comfortable about being at the Mistletoe Manor.

"Would you mind showing me around a bit? I can't wait to see my quarters," she said with an attempt to use an English accent, which caused Marie to giggle again, and made the tour a pleasant stroll for both of them.

One fascinating room after another, Kristina enjoyed the whimsical and elegant winter holiday themes that each room displayed. Marie shared with Kristina that the children of the local orphanage, Sugar Plum House were treated to visits and dinner on Christmas Eve celebrations at Mistletoe Manor. She also learned that the Bakery on Main Street shared the same name is also a benefactor that supports the operation of the children's home.

It was after entering the Essence Suite that she no longer thought it to be a humorous idea of her having quarters. Kristina gasped in awe and pinched her own arm. She stood frozen until she emotionally defrosted enough to move about the enormous stately bedroom.

She vaguely remembered Marie excusing herself but knew that her exit indeed occurred during the initial state of stupor.

Kristina's eyes traveled every inch of uniqueness that these quarters offered. From the double queen canopy bed covered with a white-satin comforter with a gold poinsettia print border, a crystal chandelier that reminded her of a wish-upon-a-star work of art she had read in a storybook, and the sitting area facing the window with a plush white couch with furry red, white, and gold throw pillows fully mesmerized her.

The fireplace in the bedroom was a luxurious touch, she thought. Having the fire going was as impressive as the bubble bath awaiting her in the oversized golden claw foot tub and silky white pajamas, matching bathrobe, and plush towels on the settee. She put her hand in the bath water and felt its warmth that convinced her that the house staff were like elves because she didn't notice the presence of whom it would take to accomplish her accommodation preparation to the level presented to her.

Kristina surrendered to the moment, and the experience then submerged herself into the lavender scented bath until her head was completely under. She held her breath as the events of the day, faces and places she saw, and oddly, thoughts of her parents flashed across her mind's eye, like a morning matinee. Kristina re-emerged with genuine openness to spend the next five days tapping into the Essence of Jolly.

CHAPTER SIX

NOT SO EASY PEAZY

T o awaken to the view of the sunrise through the frosted pine branches that lined portions of the mountains was indeed an enjoyable picturesque experience that Kristina doubted that anyone would ever get tired of seeing.

Not only was Kristina surprised to see that the luggage she had left at the Jolly Inn was sitting by the door, catching her eye as she stretched, was a rolled-up mint green exercise mat along with spandex yoga gear laid out on a chaise lounge chair that she did not see last night.

Fifteen minutes later she had her ear pods in and midway to downward dog. Fifty minutes later she inhaled deeply, bowed and bid Namaste to the universe before indulging in the dual head steam shower.

The thoughts that filled her head as the water pellets massaged every muscle continued as she stood before the vanity mirror wrapped in the luxuriously soft bath towel. She towel-dried her hair, allowing her wavy curls to reset naturally as she pondered her purpose of being in Jolly. She wondered if too much of a good thing without putting in the effort and hard work was indeed a benefit because that had not been the way she navigated her life thus far.

Kristina reminded herself that her effort moving forward was to explore Jolly as she would normally do in any difficult situation. She decided that she would do some research of her own and come up with a hypothesis, test it, then determine a theory. Her role in the Essence succession was predetermined by the choice of another, but she appreciated that the acceptance of that role was to be her choice.

She went to hang her clothes in the closet and found it full of clothes in her size. It was like shopping at her personal Rodeo Drive boutique. She admired the organization of color coding and the separation from formal to casual. She didn't see one item there that she didn't like. From scarves to shoes, she was fully enamored.

At the end of the walk-in closet that presented more like a dressing room, was an ornately carved, 7 feet high, 5 feet wide, double-door, wooden wardrobe that didn't quite match the aesthetics of the room. Feeling compelled to examine the unique bureau closer, she touched the grooved-out handle on the right-side door and immediately felt a similar sensation that she experienced when she touched the front doorknob when she arrived at Mistletoe Manor.

Hanging before her were 7 red velvet hooded capes trimmed in white fur. There were two boxes that sat on the floor of the wardrobe: one wooden, one jeweled. Kristina gave into her feelings of apprehension and resisted the urge to open either box. She closed the doors of the wardrobe and quickly dressed in a pair of denim blue jeans and a white cashmere sweater that she had brought with her. She pulled on her furry boots that matched her fashionable earmuff headband to complete her winter vacay ensemble and headed out of her suite on an adventure to find the kitchen that she did not recall seeing on her late-night tour without ringing the intercom for Marie's assistance.

Following her nose, that instantly caught wind of the scent of culinary delightfulness, she made it through the maze of beautiful Christmas decorations to a grand kitchen that reminded her of a mini bakery, a gingerbread bakery. Kristina was pleased to see organic life alongside all of the ornamental exhibits; it was a pleasant feeling; as too was watching 3 chefs dressed in white with hats joyfully singing while preparing food. They didn't hear her enter the room. She stood silently enjoying the moment until a series of three hand claps silenced the room, halting all activities.

A short round-faced woman, dressed in the same black and white attire that Marie wore last night commanded attention. The chefs quickly stood in formation behind her.

"Good morning, Dr. Rosario," she greeted.

"Good morning. And please, it's Kristina."

"Very well, Ms. Kristina. My name is Rose. I am the East Wing manager. These are your team of Chefs, Tola, Thomas, and Ben."

"Nice to meet you all. It smells simply lovely in here."

"I hope that you rested well last night and that your accommodations were acceptable. May I start your day with a cup of coffee or juice?" asked Rose.

"I would love a cup of coffee, Rose. And yes, my quarters are phenomenal thank you. Thank you to the house-staff for the attention allotted to me. I'm extremely appreciative."

"It is our privilege and an honor indeed to welcome our new Essence. Would you like to have coffee brought to you in the dining room, ma'am?"

"Um... If you don't mind, I'd like to spend more time here, amongst you all. My mother always said that the heart of a home was the kitchen, so I'd like to get to know the heart first."

"Certainly, and how about a gingerbread muffin to go with your coffee?" she asked with a smile and wink.

"Now you are speaking right to my heart, Rose."

Kristina walked over to the bench window seating in the breakfast nook of the kitchen where she sat wide-eyed in fascination watching the chefs work on the largest Gingerbread house she had ever seen. Although she had only seen it at night, she realized that the gingerbread house was a replica of Mistletoe Manor decorated for the Christmas Holiday sitting upon a wheeled table.

"Chefs, this creation is magnificent!" Kristina exclaimed. They were pleased that she thought so.

"The children look forward to it every year, even though it is significantly smaller than years ago when the Christmas Gala was the biggest celebration of the year," Rose said as she sat a pearl white porcelain cup and saucer with a metallic red trim in front of her, along with a small matching coffee pot, and a platter of assorted baked goods.

"Children? Christmas Gala?" Kristina inquired.

"Yes, the Christmas Gala started out as a fundraiser for the children at the orphanage but grew to become the mega event of the year. Celebrities would come from all over to attend. Jolly also made annual donations to several children's hospitals across the state with the excess proceeds raised."

"So, was Peazy like their benefactor of sorts?"

"The children were not just special to Madam Peazy, the children of Jolly are dear to everyone. Each child is very special. Each child has a destined purpose, as do we all. But…since losing Madam, the donors don't make an appearance or even send donations like they use to. Tourism is at an all-time low mainly because the celebration just stopped and the invitations to the charity gala were cancelled. Let's say that the people have just not been…jolly."

"When I arrived, it looked like the town was gearing up for the holidays."

"That's the thing Madam Kristina, Jolly is not a seasonal place. Well, it didn't use to be. Jolly is a collective of people with goodness in their hearts who dwell on gifted land from the Serrano people, that is sacred but once was stolen and covered with blood and tears of the indigenous because of hate and greed. Jolly was gifted for goodness and goodwill to thrive eternally. Later as the land and people healed came the light and the gift of Essence which binds us all. So, what many thinks may be a whimsical theme in the way that we live all year around is actually capturing the one time of year that people of all nations around the world manage to find some kindness and desire to share goodwill."

"When you say all year round, do you mean like Christmas themes every day of the year; 365 days of lights, trees, candy canes, and the whole nine yards of garland?"

"Yes indeed Dr. Rosario. We believe that human beings are a version of their better selves one time of year during the season of Christmas. So, in Jolly, we embrace that feeling all year so that people outside of our community can come to reset in a place that celebrates goodwill to others every day."

"Wow, I guess that I wasn't even close to comprehending the significance, but I still don't quite understand my role in any of this."

"All I can say Ms. Kristina, is that the word of the arrival of the new Essence has spread throughout our town and to the neighboring communities and has sprung hope to the residents of Jolly. The essence of Christmas is with us all year around and gets elevated as we really amp things up during the season that the rest of the world tends to celebrate and acknowledge the big guy or the memory of the little guy who is really bigger than the big guy, if you know what I mean.

"Yes Rose. I do. Now when you say that the people have hope because of the new Essence, are you referring to me?"

"Yes Ma'am. Madam Peazy always said that you would come some day and bring our town into the new Millennium and things would be grander than ever before."

"She said that; did she?"

"Yes Ma'am, she did."

"Well, did she happen to say how that was supposed to happen?"

"No Ma'am, she did not."

"I don't know about any of this. I mean, I am basically here until the end of the week. Certainly, she had an apprentice or an assistant that kept records or details."

"You may want to ask Marvin Lee. He should be here… momentarily," Rose replied as she looked at the pocket watch she pulled from her apron pocket.

As predicted, Marvin Lee enters the kitchen of the Manor carrying a large cardboard box that he sat on the counter. The 3 chefs gathered cheerfully reaching into the box retrieving its contents.

"Please thank the children for the fresh herbs. I have a basket of pastries and freshly baked bread for them," said Chef Tola, as he headed into the butler's pantry to retrieve the treats.

"Sure thing Chef," Marvin Lee yelled out, then turned to give Rose a hug. "Sorry I'm a little late, we had a new colt make his entrance this morning."

"How exciting! So, what did we name the little fella?"

"The kids named him Marshmallow," he chuckled. He is chocolate brown, just like his mother, Cocoa, except he has a white square patch right in the center of his head."

"Hence the name Marshmallow!" Rose joined in laughter. "Can I get you a cup of coffee?"

"I can never say no to your special blend, Rose. But just a quick cup. I have to get back to the camp. We have a lot to do to prepare for the games this week.

"Why don't I make two 2-go-cups and you can take Madame Kristina out to the ranch and show her around."

"Kristina?" he questioned with a grimace.

Marvin Lee was so distracted, he did not notice that she was present. He looked behind him and saw her sitting in the nook area, sipping on a cup of coffee.

Noticing the look of sheer surprise on his face, Kristina waved at him with an awkward smile.

"Dr. Rosario," Marvin managed to say after clearing his throat. He did not have time to process his mixed emotions, yet alone fully hiding them. "I thought you went back to L.A."

"Nope. I decided to stick around and get to know the place, the people, and more about Pamelia, which I'm told you could help me with."

"Um…yeah. I suppose I can do that," he answered, clearing his throat again."

"Let me run and grab my jacket and scarf."

Rose suddenly appeared not only with two styrofoam cups, but with Kristina's Jacket and scarf draped across her arm. Rose met Kristina's smile with a smile and a wink. Marvin Lee stepped in as a gentleman and assisted Kristina with putting on her jacket. He placed the tan knit scarf around her neck.

"I'm glad you stayed, Doc."

"I'm glad I stayed."

"Let me get the door, my lady," he said in his best Bishop impersonation.

"Thank you, kind sir," she replied with a giggle at the resemblance.

CHAPTER SEVEN

THE REINDEER RANCH

Upon passing the entrance of the wooden fence post onto the Reindeer Ranch, Kristina felt as if she had just been transported into an oil painting that she remembered seeing and admired on a wall in Mistletoe Manor.

The snow blanketed the fields for as far as she could see in each direction, outlined by the deciduous black oaks and maples with their naked branches standing strong and tall meeting the rich blue morning sky. The enormous bushy pines with snow draped on the foliage like a mink shawl was indeed a spectacular focal point as an eye-catching border.

The shelter structures blended nicely into the backdrop of nature's rural Winterland. Marvin Lee pointed out the 2-story red barn, two stables, and a substantial greenhouse. Kristina was fascinated at the sight of some mini log cabins with porches along a path that led to the rather large log cabin that had a wrapped-around porch with several rocking chairs. There was a trailing cloud of smoke prancing in the air from the chimney top that signaled that they had arrived to an intriguing destination.

Instinctively, before the pickup truck could slowly roll to a complete stop, the front door of the main cabin flew open and a dozen kids and young adults ran out and down the five stairs then surrounded the vehicle.

They were all jumping with joy and were all speaking with excitement at the same time in an effort to share some news with Marvin Lee. Once he greeted them back with equal enthusiasm, he pointed to one person to be the spokesperson for the news that they were anxious to share. A young boy, around 10, announced that the Christmas Rose bloomed this morning. Marvin Lee met the news with a group hug and a series of high-five hand slaps. He instructed one of the kids to grab the basket of bread and baked treats from the rear cabin of the truck. The group cheered and ran back into the house.

Thinking that she had exited the passenger side of the truck unnoticed, Kristina was introduced to the six camp counselors who stayed behind out of curiosity and a formal introduction.

Kristina soon saw that Reindeer Ranch was more than just an amazing winter youth camp for agriculture studies and an animal haven. She could feel the energy and looked forward to seeing more.

"Hey guys. I'd like you to meet Dr. Kristina Rosario, from Los Angeles. Dr. Rosario, these are our camp counselors, Victor, Don, Coop, Dash, Q, and our guy with the sniffles, Rudy," said jokingly as the young man with rhinitis runs up late to the gathering.

"Hey, I get windburn easily," he replied pointing to his nose with both index fingers."

"And I bet you had spicy chili for breakfast too." Marvin Lee countered with a smirk and a squinted eye.

"Okay, you got me, one small bowl." The guys all laughed, including Rudy knowing spicy chili makes his nose redder than normal.

"Please call me Kristina. It is a pleasure to meet you all. And Rudy, I get windburn sometimes too and I have a great remedy that will help you with that. Plus, my mother makes the spiciest tortas abogados. Mmm so good."

"Oh doc, I like her," said Rudy as he extended his elbow bent arm to escort her into the main cabin. "So, tell me more about this tortas ahogadas."

"Tortas abogados," she laughed and repeated slowly. "Well, it's bread drenched in a spicy sauce. Mmm so good."

Rudy's taste buds began salivating, while Kristina inhaled deeply to enjoy the blended cool air mixed with the smoky aroma of a wood burning fire. The pleasant char smell intensified the closer they got to the door. She noticed the oversized fireplace hearth and the dancing flames that emitted a slightly sweet note that gave a sense of coziness and nostalgia as soon as she crossed the threshold. She politely curtsied to excuse her escort; however, his bow was interrupted as someone playfully snatched Rudy's hat and ran off into another room. She thought to herself that Jolly had quite a few gentlemen, and Rudy was a contender as her favorite.

Kristina walked closer to the fireplace to bathe in its warmth. She looked around the rather large communal space that had a charmingly rustic decor of three plush cushioned sofas anchoring the fireplace and 6 oversized chairs paired off around the room in conversational clusters. The unique carpentry of the wood cocktail and side tables, large wicker baskets of throw blankets, board game boxes, books and indigenous accents throughout the room added to its vibe of lived-in coziness.

But it was the oil painting of a larger than life sized Native American with a tear spilling from his eye, down his face, then onto the ground of a mountain of pine trees below him that caused her pause. She felt the artist captured a pain that was of an intense nature that the ground below him absorbed.

Managing to pull herself away from the painting, Kristina followed the lively and youthful sounds of laughter and chatter to a spacious country chic kitchen where the children congregated around a 10-foot butcher block island in the center of the room. Marvin Lee smiled when he saw her and waved her in. All eyes turned towards her, as she walked into the now awkwardly silent air, nervously waving hello to everyone.

"Hey everyone. Please give a warm Jolly welcome and say hello to Dr. Kristina," Marvin Lee directed.

"Hi Dr. Kristina," the children sang in unison.

"Let's go around the table and introduce yourselves."

One by one, the children gave their names and ages. It was 12-year-old Maggie who raised her hand with a question for Kristina.

"Are you a people doctor or an animal doctor like Marvin Lee?"

"Animal doctor?" Kristina looked confused over at Marvin Lee who leaned his head to the side and raised a brow.

"Maybe a cat has her tongue." The children laughed. "Dr. Kristina is a people doctor, little people. Isn't that right, Dr. Rosario?"

"I'm sorry." Kristina gathered her thoughts and regained focus on the children. "Yes, I am a doctor who specializes in babies up to young adult ages."

Two more children raised their hands. Kristina pointed at Billy and recalled his name. She remembered that he was the boy who was excited to share the news of the Christmas Rose.

"Is it true that you are the new Essence?"

Kristina saw expressions of hope on each of their faces. She wanted to be careful and considerate of her words when answering.

"Um, I am not quite sure how to answer that, Billy." She noticed the slow regression on their faces that was balancing on her every word. "I am learning a lot about how important being an Essence is right now, so I will get back to you with a definite answer later. Can someone tell me more about the Christmas Rose?"

Their faces reignited with a spark of joy at the mention of the subject. She pointed at the tallest boy. She gave a second to recall his name using her style of word association. Tall gave her Tony.

"The Christmas Rose blooms in our greenhouse right

before Christmas. Once it blooms, we go out and cut down our Christmas tree for the house." The children cheered with excitement.

"That sounds amazing," Kristina replied."

"Will you come to the Reindeer Games this week?" Billy shouted out.

"Reindeer Games?"

"Yeah, it's like the Jolly Olympics except every year," Maggie answered.

"The counselors versus the campers in flag football, snowball target throws, and a snowperson building contest," Rudy added, then blew his nose into a handkerchief.

"We didn't do it last year because we were all too sad, but now that we have a new Essence, she can judge the snow people contest!" Billy exclaimed with high energy.

"She is not the Essence stupid! We don't have anyone anymore," Shawn, an 11-year-old red-hair boy said angrily, with his arms folded across his chest.

"Hey hey now! We don't call names. You need to apologize right now. Look, I know that we all miss Peazy, but you have many people that care about each and every one of you. So, what am I? Chopped liver?" Marvin Lee interjected with humor.

"I'd love to be the judge for the snowperson contest," Kristina announced.

The children cheered and ran over to her for a group hug. Kristina. She passed out high-five hand slaps all around. The counselors instructed the children to bundle up for the Christmas tree hunt. Kristina smiled and watched them disperse individually and head outside into the snow from the large kitchen window as they tracked on foot behind 4 snowmobiles towards the wooded area of the property.

Kristina completed her tour of Reindeer Ranch with Marvin Lee first with the amazing greenhouse that was nothing short of an agricultural paradise complete with it's crown jewel, the Christmas Rose, then a quick stroll into the stables full of animals being sheltered from the harsh cold for the winter season, to lastly, watching endearingly as Marvin Lee perform a veterinary check-up on Cocoa and Marshmallow before heading back to Mistletoe Manor.

Kristina felt at that moment that her tour guide was a closed book with an obscure cover. An attractive obscure cover. She decided that she could not yield to any urge to discover all the hidden layers of Marvin Lee, hotel groundskeeper, slash ranch hand, slash youth mentor, slash Doctor of Veterinary Medicine, slash personal tour guide. She had not allowed herself to entertain the thought of getting to know a man beyond work or a casual acquaintance in a very long time.

With less than a week remaining in Jolly, she felt that she did not have the luxury of time to even consider whatever the emotional entanglement that was starting to stir within her core would even look like.

"So, Doc, I wanted to thank you again for agreeing to judge an event out at the ranch on what might actually be your last day in Jolly."

"It is my pleasure and the least that I can do, Doc."

"Ha, ha, ha, all jokes aside, but Doc is my Dad. So the Marvin Lee story is a long one about expectations that I wouldn't want to bore you with."

"I think that I am starting to understand more about expectations the hard way."

"I suppose so, Kristina…how about a tour of the Ski Lodge and Hotel tomorrow?"

"Hotel?"

"Yeah 40 rooms, big tourist area…well it used to be."

"I'd like that. How about 10:30? I need to get a run or workout in before heading out so that I can continue to ravish all of those baked goods at the manor without the guilt," she joked.

"I will pick you up at 10:30 tomorrow morning."

"It's a date…I mean, I will see you then," she tried to recover quickly.

Kristina scurried quickly from the truck to the door of Mistletoe Manor, hiding her embarrassment from the slip of the tongue that she began to over analyze in her mind every minute it parted her lips.

CHAPTER EIGHT

A JOLLY SKI LODGE

T hree outfit changes later, Kristina settled for the black fleece lined leggings and a black thigh-length turtleneck sweater. The cheetah-print fur on the brim of her knit hat matched the cheetah-print fur socks folded over the top of her ankle boots. She did a full 360 view in the tri-fold full-length mirror after dabbing her cinnamon spice matt-finish lipstick.

Thinking back on her morning run in the brisk mountain air that was intended to clear her mind, took on more mental baggage instead.

She could not shake the feeling of comfort among all of the whimsical scenery surrounding Mistletoe Manor. Kristina felt tingly inside when she took deep breaths as if every sense within her was somehow awakened and instantaneously formed a connection with Jolly. What she saw, smelled, tasted, touched, or heard was heightened.

She thought about the children out at Reindeer Ranch and Marvin Lee, the house staff at the manor; Rose, Marie, the 3 Chefs, and the Bishops back at the Inn. She was really impressed by the diversity and cohesiveness of modern, whimsical, and cultural traditions, respect, and values of indigenous people who gifted the land that the town was built upon.

Kristina vividly recalled awakening from a recurring dream since arriving to Jolly. She dreamt of a white-gloved hand, gently petting a horse with mesmerizing eyes shedding a tear. The single tear drop would land on the ground and a luminous cloud would appear. She would shortly thereafter notice a cracked snow globe suspended in air with water running out of it falling to her foot that no matter how hard she tried, she was unable to pick up and examine closer.

Although Kristina's unusual dreams were not uncommon for Kristina since she could remember even as a child, it was somewhat different these past few days. She had the same dream the night before leaving for Jolly that had to do with snow globes. Snow globes were something that she loved as a child.

Kristina had 5 ornately crafted snow globes that sat on golden bases sitting on a wall display shelf in her childhood bedroom that she received as birthday gifts at ages 6, 12, 16, 21, and 25. She always thought it was cute that her parents always denied gifting them to her. So just like what the tooth fairy left behind under her pillow when she lost her baby teeth, it was settled that Santa's gift for Christmas Eve birthdays as the explainable origin.

Kristina had decided against talking to her mother about her dream before getting on the road. Ordinarily this would be something she usually would have done, since dream interpretation was a culturally ambiguous gift that her mother practiced and believed in.

Kristina was more the scientific type. As she grew up and could relate stressful situations, sleep deprivation, and late-night television with the human subconscious in theory, but she couldn't deny that there was more to it than a mere level of entertainment that she felt listening to the alternative theory of unconscious awareness.

Kristina chuckled as she thought about a conversation that she once had with London about her dreams when they were college roommates. London's response was a tale about her uncle who carried around a pocket-sized dream book that he would use to come up with lottery numbers. London wasn't sure if there was any evidence that dreams attributed to any of his gambling wins, since statistically he lost far more than he ever won.

Suddenly, something dawned on Kristina, that she had almost forgotten about. The snow globe that she received on her 25th birthday was actually cracked. Almost all of the fluid had seeped out and the snow village was not as enchanting as the others in her collection. Kristina recalled her mother being as disappointed as she pretended to be as surprised by the content when she opened the box. Her mother offered to find someone who makes or repairs snow globes, but Kristina told her not to worry, but when she suggested that she file an insurance claim with the Post Office to cover damages, once again, her mother denied being the sender. Kristina said that she only suggested it because of the gold base and intricate design and details similar to an expensive Faberge egg, she knew these were not the average souvenir shop globes.

Although she decided to play along, by suggesting that she was going to file a complaint with Santa, she was disappointed with herself for not taking the time out of her work schedule to take care of something that once meant so much to her. She knew there was more than a fraction of truth in her co-workers who challenged her to balance her life.

Kristina's train of thought was interrupted by a knock at the bedroom door, announcing that her ride had arrived.

One last mirror check was performed and a satisfactory wink to herself was given approving her final look right down to the school-girl smile.

◆ ◆ ◆

The ride was quieter than Kristina had expected. She was not her talkative self. Her giddiness was a new emotion for her. She felt Marvin Lee's eyes on her and felt some of the slightest swerves were results of anything longer than a glance. They both relaxed as he began to point out sights along the way to their destination.

Marvin Lee started the tour in the truck and said that they would finish the latter part on foot because the weather report indicated a snowstorm. He said that the residents were excited as it was revealed that they were behind on snowfall for the season and has been that way since Peazy departed. He went on to say that unlike many ski resorts, they have never had to use artificial snow, but they were wondering if they would have to. He seemed happily confident that the weather was favorable conditions for Jolly.

The tour of the Lodge and ski resort certainly did not disappoint. Kristina thought that with a few cosmetic updates, the potential would be nothing short of spectacular. But it was much of the natural beauty all around her that enveloped her heart. She thought to herself, if this place was a person, she would be falling in love at first sight.

Giant Snowflakes ceremoniously poured from the noontime skies. Layer after layer, the gusty winds were navigating each flake to take its rightful resting place upon the earth and softly embed into their position within nature's glacial quilt.

The view of Mistletoe Mountain up close to Jolly's Ski Lodge was as breathtaking as it was from downtown and the surrounding areas. Kristina thought to herself that the morning view from any of the 40 rooms of Jolly's One Season Hotel was a sight worth spending a night seeing.

As the slopes were clearing of skiers due to the forecast of inclement weather, an announcement could be heard that the ski lift was temporarily closed. Kristina realized that the lights that she saw from a distance back at the Manor along the mountainside at night, were actually the gondolas that looked like miniature Christmas tree lights.

Surrounded by the fanciful unique lodging structures of a dozen gingerbread designed cottages uniquely named after the 12 Christmas gifts from Cottage One-Partridge all the way through to Cottage Twelve- Drummers. There were four larger chalets that housed larger groups. The chalets were more elegant than whimsical in nature with floor to ceiling windows, antler chandeliers, and rustic chic decor. Each Chalet came with a personal chef and personal planner package for individualized experiences. She thought the chalets would definitely be something that her and her friend group could do if she made time to enjoy and smell the winter roses.

She thought it beyond adorable watching the St. Bernard

pups frolicking in the snow. They played near the First Aid Station located at the junction of the Y path that led to either the entrance to the Chimney Hill slope which was the beginner and family friendly slope; or to the Old Grinch Mount, which was designed for the more advanced level skiers.

As Kristina and Marvin Lee decided to cut their tour short to shelter in place at the hotel until the winter snowfall subsided, suddenly out of nowhere, they appeared to be under attack by a miniature army of kids who laughed and snickered at each pound of snow ammunition that landed. Their aim landed more shots on Marvin Lee; however, Kristina could not resist joining in on the friendly snowball fight after feeling the soft but cold impact on the back of her arm. Marvin Lee and Kristina ducked behind an evergreen bush for cover and began to strategize.

"Friends of yours, I gather?" she inquired.

"You could say so. Although it is an annual ritual that marks the start of The Reindeer Games, they catch me off guard every time. One day I will get the upper hand," he chuckled.

"Well, this may be the day, my friend. I may not be used to snow, but you are looking at a 3 time, 3-years in a row, High School championship winning softball pitcher! Let's get em' this time!" she charged.

Their strategy won the war as 2 kids retreated and the other 2 surrendered, giving Marvin Lee his first victory in a few years.

The snowball battle was witnessed and cheered on by some of the guests and staff from the lobby. The victors were greeted with applause, warm blankets, and hot cider when they entered the hotel. Kristina enjoyed seeing the playful side of Marvin Lee.

She stared at him as if she was attempting to capture that very moment in hope not to forget as she was pulled away by Mya, a kind manager directing her to a hospitality suite where she could dry-off and change into something comfortable while her wet clothes were laundered.

On her way to the suite, she smiled as she noticed guests gathered around the fireplace sipping on their choice of hot or frozen cocoa while engaging in a fun-filled group trivia activity.

Kristina donned a loaned winter sweater that fit her size but not necessarily her usual fashion; however, she felt rather comfortable and cheerful in the snowflake motif and found it fitting for the occasion.

She stared out of the window and watched as the wind tossed waves of white dust that crystallized the resort's grounds.

"Could I really?" she asked herself aloud.

"Could you really what?"

Startled, Kristina turned away from the window towards the voice, unfolding her arms and placing one hand on her chest.

Standing in the doorway of the adjoining room to the suite, stood Marvin Lee. He was barefoot and shirtless, wearing fresh dry jeans. His raven-black hair was wet, wavy, and loose. Not tied back in the loose man-bun he usually wore. She went from startled to mesmerized as she noticed the tattoo that covered his muscular upper arm and chest of a majestic horse towering a pony. The colors of its mane and Native American emblem were beautiful and breathtaking against his natural sun-kiss bronze skin. She felt as if the horse's head moved with the twitch of his pecs and the rise of his chest with the inspiration from his breathing. Kristina was rendered speechless for an amount of time that she could not calculate.

"Dr. Rosario, are you alright?" Marvin Lee asked with concern.

"So, what will it take for you to just call me Kristina?"

"I did, like 3 times. Kristina, are you OK?"

Now embarrassed, she answered, "Yes. It's just that I didn't know that I wasn't alone," she recovered.

"Oh, sorry about that, I assumed Mya mentioned that I usually hang out here every now and then. Believe it or not, Peazy loved the view of the Mistletoe Mountain from this suite most in all of Jolly," he said as he walked over to the window pointing. "She designed the gingerbread cottages. She really loved gingerbread, he said with a smile as he gazed at the buildings.

His smile broke her stare in trance at his manly physique. She still didn't look out of the window. She kept her eyes on his handsome profile which captivated her attention. His smile began to slowly retreat to its neutral position and his eyes began to coat with a wet glaze.

"You miss her, don't you?

"I don't think I will ever stop, he sighed, looking at the horizon. If you only knew how important Jolly and every person, animal, or thing was to her..." He took a deep breath before retreating to silence.

"Why don't you tell me?"

"I wouldn't want to bore you."

"No, seriously, I really want to know more about my benefactor. I'd love for you to share with me your memories of her." She reached up and gently turned his strong jaw towards her. "This place is magical and the longer I am here, the harder it is for me to even consider my life in LA. But there are so many mixed emotions and unanswered questions about me, about Pamelia Zavala, about Essence…and about you."

"Me?"

"Yes you, Dr. Marvin Lee Mass Jr. From the looks of things outside, I think we will be here for a while. I am going to call down to the front desk and ask Mya to send us some lunch and more of that delicious cider. So go get prepared for story time, she said shooing him back towards the open adjoining room door.

"It sounds like you are taking charge of this tour?"

"Correct. It's a city gal thing, I suppose. And Marvin Lee…"

"Yes?"

"A shirt is optional. Just saying," she jokingly smirked.

CHAPTER NINE

REINDEER GAMES

Serving as an event Judge at The Reindeer Games was such an honor for Kristina. Familiar faces from all of the shops on Main Street lent to the sense of belonging that cloaked Kristina during the festivities. The waves from the crowd directed at her specifically made her feel like spectators were there for a glimpse of her as well as the games themselves. But after waking up tucked tightly by a plush blanket on the sofa in the hospitality suite of Jolly's One Season Hotel, she had a reciprocal smile for each and everyone. She harbored a new appreciation for their plight.

Kristina was full of ideas to help this mourning town. Her imagination was overflowing.

She left a lengthy message for her bestie before dawn and knew that London Haney had the power and connections to implement and elevate her plans.

The larger than life-sized grin and 2 thumbs up from Attorney Randall West, in the crowd was confirmation that things were well underway.

The youth and camp counselors were neck and neck most of the events like the relay toy sack race, the sleigh race, and dodge snowball, but the youth team pulled out the tie breaker win with the Snowperson contest for originality. She admitted that brownie points were awarded because the larger snowwoman with a red towel cape that had tree branch hands, holding a snowball, surrounded by several snow children tugged at her heartstrings for the win.

Kristina announced that she would be heading over to the Tinsel Tavern for the best Shepherd's Pie that she had ever tasted and hoped to speak with as many of the merchants on Main Street about revitalizing Jolly's Christmas Gala.

The joyous looks on the faces in the crowd and hugs shared among them with excitement validated that she was doing the right thing.

Even Marvin Lee cast a sincere look of happiness as the kids hung all over him while jumping for joy. Randall West threw her another big smile and two thumbs up once again.

She felt her pocket vibrate and recognized it as her cellphone. She looked down and saw that it was London and put the phone back into her pocket. She excused herself and scurried to the stables for privacy to return London's call.

"Hey Bestie, give me the good news."

"Well, do you want the good news or great news first?"

"Whichever says you were able to get everything done on the list."

"Oh okay, the good news it is. I did it all and more. I just reserved all 4 Chalets with celebrity A-listers and their families. Do you know that several Old Hollywood Royalties have been there; even as children? I heard that there used to be this Willy Wonka type vibe with golden tickets or invitations that came to guests. So, I took that idea, and my team ran with it. It turns out that typical Hollywood all want in on anything that is exclusive, and the buzz is trending. I suspect that the hotel will be lucky if they have any vacancies. So, we have private transportation arranged thanks to the help of a rather sexy lawyer that makes me feel real Jolly if you can pick up what a sista is throwing down..."

"Another time Londy."

"Yeah indeed. Now there are 8 celebrity designers, carpenters, and builders from the Real Home Channel Network that will be arriving tomorrow and donating time and materials for 2 days. The 2 chefs and ice sculptor that you specifically asked for all agreed to fly in. And finally, the staffing agency is offering hospitality staff for all the help that you may need."

"Wow Londy, you did your thing as I knew you would."

"Was there any doubt Tina?"

"Not even a little. So now if that was just the good news, then now I am curious to know what news is better than that?"

"Just the news that we have been hoping for and waiting for. Kristina you are now officially the newest cast member on Practicing Hollywood!!!" London screamed loud.

Kristina removed the phone from her ear. She took a deep breath, then exhaled emotionlessly before putting her on speakerphone.

"What is wrong Tina? Are you not excited? This is what you have worked so hard for and have wanted for so long. Right?"

"I suppose so, but now I am not so sure if that is what I want anymore."

"What are you saying sis? Are you throwing all of this away for a little house in the snow?"

"It's a rather big house in the snow."

"Are you serious? Looks like I need to get up there sooner rather than later. So how much does a sexy youth camp director and veterinarian have to do with your decision? And be honest."

"Nothing London. I don't think he even likes me or wants me around half the time. Maybe LA is my present and future after all, so let's just wait and talk about it when you get here."

Kristina heard the barn door close, then ran over to see if anyone was there. She didn't see that Marvin Lee had overheard part of her conversation. He heard her say that LA was her present and her future. Kristina didn't see him duck out and head behind the stables out of sight to process his emotions. She didn't hear him storm off saying that he hated allowing himself to be vulnerable with her last night when he knew her type.

She ended her call with London and looked forward to seeing her best friend in 2 days.

She heard the barn door again and this time saw Randall West enter the stable area. He still had a big smile.

"Hey there Randall. I just got off the phone with London."

"I tell you; she is an amazing woman. She almost had me ready to do a one-man art show, he laughed. I don't know about being an artist full time in Jolly, but I sure hope to see a bit more of Ms. Haney and how does she say it, if you get what I'm putting down?" he said laughing.

"Oh, I get what you are putting down Randall."

"Oh, Marvin Lee mentioned that you were in here and I wanted to offer you a ride over to the Tinsel Tavern since he had something last minute come up."

"I would love to hitch a ride with you, kind sir," she replied and grabbed hold of his extended arm.

"You know, I agree with you. They do have the best Shepherd's Pie."

"Yes indeed."

CHAPTER TEN

THE RED CAPE CRUSADE

The sound of hammers and power tools echoed in the air. Fresh coats of paint, Christmas lights, and decorations were being placed in every space available. Jolly was re-awakened after 25 long months of grieving. Kristina felt alive and connected after years of feeling incomplete.

Kristina's vision was coming together to spruce things up but not change the organic character of Jolly. The large outdoor ice-skating rink in the city center was a big highlight that both young and old looked forward to.

The upgraded renovations at the ski lodge were well underway and guests are expected to enjoy the best of themed tourism with personalized hospitality and without the commercialization overtones.

The banquet hall at The One Seasons Hotel was being transformed into the most amazing dining experience for the guests and residents of Jolly for this year's Christmas Gala.

Roasted Chestnut station, S'mores station, Hot Cocoa and Apple Cider booths were constructed on 3 areas of the resort.

The Santa Helicopter Pad received a fresh coat of glow-in-the-dark red painted H and red and white striped painted borders.

The shops along Main Street looked extraordinarily welcoming and each had window displays that would tempt the average strolling passersby to come inside. Unless it was the Train display because one could become frost bitten watching every detail for hours on end.

It was Kristina who was redesigned when she finally visited the orphanage, The Sugar Plum House. The little faces. Their eyes. Their hearts. Their smiles. Their tears. The essence of Jolly was not just the title of an Essence.

Even the engraved bronze plague at the Town Hall City's Center began to take on a new meaning in its entirety. It read:

Upon This Gifted And Sacred Land Of Pines, We, The Citizens Of Jolly Represent Goodness In All People From Around The World. We Are All Beneficiaries Of Essence, Who United Will Continue To Spread The Gift Of Love, Peace, And Goodwill To All Mankind

There were oil paintings on the wall of beautiful women in the red velvet capes interacting with children of all ages holding an amber glowing orb or sphere object. Just being in that space, and in the presence of the adorable children in need of someone who cared ignited something inside of Kristina that caused a glow when they gathered around her in a group hug circle. A glow that brightened her and the room. It was exponentially bigger than the doorknob and baby rattle glow. Mystic magic filled the air all around her. Oddly, a brief but noticeable breath of pine filled her nostrils.

Kristina savored in thought every moment she spent with the children. She enjoyed their wide-eye responses to the gala plans. They were particularly curious about the Gingerbread House display. They loved Gingerbread houses and were excited about seeing the 12 gingerbread cottages at the ski resort. Most of all, they were excited about being a part of a surprise gift during the Gala celebration.

By the time the chauffeur got them back to the Manor, Kristina was famished. A good old Turkey with cranberry sauce on one side toasted bread like her mother used to make filled her head, but she would be appreciative of anything that either of the 3 chefs would have prepared for her. She almost felt guilty for even thinking about them having to consider her meals on top of their task of creating their grand scaled Gingerbread House and cake.

Kristina was even more excited that London was arriving today instead of tomorrow as planned. Brian left early this morning to head down to Los Angeles to pick her up. Having her for moral support was exactly what the doctor ordered for herself. Knowing that she was bringing a designer with her that specializes in Christmas decorating to help oversee last minute details was a bonus and needed aspect to bring everything together.

Kristina could see as the car made its way through the estate gates that even Mistletoe Manor was getting a little spruced up from what Kristina had already thought to be beautiful. She was pleased by all that she saw.

The driver, Titus, exited and hurriedly walked over to open Kristina's door. She grabbed as many bags as she could before heading inside. She was appreciative and knew that Titus would get the rest and those in the trunk of course.

Before Kristina could reached for the door knob, the front door opened wide. To her pleasant surprise, there standing in the doorway was London with her arms wide open. Kristina dropped all of her shopping bags and threw her arms around her friend. They hugged each other tightly. Gradually, the initial screams of excitement began to mellow out enough to form conversation.

"Hey gorgeous. You are a sight for sore eyes!"

"Oh London, I am so happy to see you. I have so much to tell you."

"Well, you certainly held out about this amazing house! It is next level awesome, Bestie. We haven't even seen it all and have been here for over 2 hours."

"Oh, that's right, the designer you brought. Where is he?"

"He is a she...and she is tidying up. Rose has set us up with a little snack, so I think she will be down shortly," London confirmed as they headed towards the kitchen.

"Oh Chef, how did you..." Kristina exclaimed, with wide eyes, gasping and placing both hands over her mouth.

"Chef was gracious enough to let me take over this fabulous kitchen," said the familiar voice behind her. Kristina could barely turn around and began to sob with pure happiness.

"Kristina, may I present your Christmas Decorator extraordinaire, Senora Delores Rosario," London manages to say, holding back emotions.

"Madre!!!"

"Princessa!"

Mother and daughter embraced and wiped each other's tears away. Kristina looked over again at the tray of quarter-cut turkey and cranberry sauce sandwiches and rested her head on her mother's shoulder before composing herself enough for them to sit and dine.

"Ok, Londy, you scored 50,000 points on this surprise."

"Come on now Tina, who do you know better than Mama Rosario for the oversight of your Christmas vision."

"Yes, but I was expecting my parents the day of the Gala to see it all together."

"Nonsense, Kristina. I would have wanted nothing more than to help you instead of just being a guest."

"You are right Mami. I am overjoyed right now just having 2 of my favorite people in the entire world by my side. I have so much to share with you both, but right now I'm starving, and I want to show you everything."

"I can't wait Tina, but at some point, I am going to leave you and your project manager to do the Christmas deco thingy, while I go see a handsome lawyer about brief...I mean a brief."

"Oh, London, I think we both understand what you mean," said Mama Rosario.

The ladies laughed and enjoyed a wonderful lunch.

CHAPTER ELEVEN

TOUGH DECISIONS

With all of the preparations, it suddenly dawned on Kristina that she had not seen Marvin Lee in a few days. Thinking back, she realized that it had been since the Reindeer Games. She was hoping to see him before tonight's festivities since he was instrumental to the clarity of her enlightenment of just how special the land and all of its inhabitants united contributes to the uniqueness of Jolly far beyond the themed atmosphere. She wanted to thank him personally for everything.

She looked down at her watch and inhaled before smiling. She knew that the special guests had arrived and would be out at the Reindeer Ranch an hour before dusk. She had gone over her speech several times and was still nervous and somewhat apprehensive about disappointing people who held her to binding standards. She kept repeating a portion of the speech until it slid off of her tongue confidently, and without tears.

"Being true to oneself has to be the foundation that everything else that is accomplished in life depends on. Sometimes making wrong decisions and having regrets build character. But when life throws you opportunities, you will have to reach up and catch the ones that keep you true to who you are and what you have worked for and allow what you don't catch to be a blessing and an opportunity for someone else equally deserving. So, without regret, I sadly have to say goodbye."

Until the tires came to a complete stop from the ride over to the ranch, she had not managed to get through her speech once without tearing up. She anticipated looks of disappointment that she couldn't shake.

As Titus opened the rear passenger door, she leaned forward and caught a glance of Marvin Lee's face from a distance. It had a flat effect, and she wasn't able to read him. He was looking off in another direction. But as she stood tall after exiting the car, their eyes met. Their eyes spoke softly in their own silent language. They both inhaled and nodded at each other before she was carted away by Titus to a ceremonial teepee to meet the tribe elders. Marvin Lee followed behind them dressed in the appropriate tribal attire. Kristina stopped to wave to the crowd of villagers who were gathered around an enormous circumference bonfire before disappearing into the opening being held by the tribesmen.

Titus stayed outside waiting while Kristina and Marvin Lee entered the sacred space inside of the ceremonial teepee that would serve as the bridge for the physical and the spiritual realms.

Katrina remained silent and respectful of the traditions and rituals as she entered what was considered the womb of Mother Earth. She looked around in awe at the symbolic Ledger art of the constellation and hundreds of pine trees on the buffalo-hide canvased walls and how the art seemed to have life and movement with the flicker of light cast from the fire in the pit in the center of the teepee.

Kristina noticed the space to be particularly warm, considering it was a canvased shelter on a shoveled snow ground. She saw that there were seven grass mats positioned in a circle around the fire pit. All but two were occupied by men without shirts but in tribal fabric. They all seemed to have animal tattoos similar to Marvin Lee's. Her mind drifted back to visions of him standing in the dimly lit hotel room glowing. The voice of a tribesman disrupted the trance of her revisited memory.

"Essence Kristina, greetings. I am Daniel Wolfe and we are Maara'yam; People of Maara, or as you would say, The People of the Pines." They both bowed their heads. He extended his hand towards the larger, more authoritative looking tribesman with a unique headrest. "I present to you Chief Asa Manning of the Serrano people, also known as the Yuhaaviatam, welcome to the ancestral territory gifted by Kruktat our Creator."

Kristina bowed her head while extending her hands palm up, giving respect and honor to the tribe leader.

"To whom among you have you selected?" asked their greeter.

Kristina, still silent, looks down towards the ground and steps backward, allowing Marvin Lee to be positioned forward.

"Hamiinat, Nei'ka' werrawerra'n

Maarrênga'twichi' - *Hello, Speak to me in Serrano!*"

"Hamiinat. I am Marvin Lee Mass Jr., Son of the land. Chosen by the current Essence, as was my father and my grandfather before me.

The Shaman came over, hummed and circled Marvin Lee with smoke from an artifact. Kristina looked up and noticed that the tribesman removing the blanket draped over Marvin Lee was in fact his father, Dr. Mass Sr. Then with his upper body exposed he walked over to the center of the teepee and joined the other tribesmen and knelt down on an open mat before the firepit.

The flap of the tent opened once again, and Kristina was led out of the ceremonial space joining the others united at dusk for this ritual of blessing the land and its inhabitants.

Kristina shed tears and picked back up in thought where she left off minutes ago. She thought back to the night she last spent with Marvin Lee.

She learned that night as they talked until she fell asleep, of his family history and how his father and grandfather were both protectors of the Essence through Pamelia and her predecessor Essence through Gladys. Protectors are appointed positions given to an individual who is honorable and true of good nature to all living and non-living upon the land. Marvin Lee could only be honored with the title by the interim or new Essence.

Kristina did not have to be able to read Marvin Lee like a page of an ordinary man, because he was an extraordinary open book about all that he cared for. She had never met anyone like him and highly doubted that type of man could exist in the world that she lived in. She decided after hearing him and truly seeing him as the protective horse spirit to grant him his place amongst his ancestral lineage to the Yuhaaviatam Tribe, regardless of her decision to stay in Jolly or return to Los Angeles.

She thought about her staff and co-workers at the Hospital, Jasper, her concierge, and his wife's delicious cookies. She took a deep breath and looked over at her bestie, her mother and father who arrived last night, and knew exactly at that moment what she had to do.

The words began to stick in her dry throat as the drums stopped beating and the people stopped dancing. It was her signal to begin her address to the people of Jolly. Her level of nervousness was higher than she could ever recall; much higher than sitting for her medical board exam, she thought. She looked out at the faces in the crowd. Her heart warmed seeing the youth and camp counselors with their gloved hands grasping in hope. Kristina knew that she had to snatch the proverbial Band-Aid off.

"Citizens of Jolly. On this blessed and sacred land, I come to you with sincere gratitude for your kindness and for your acceptance of me at face value. You all have welcomed me in a way that I have only known once, but a welcome that has lasted a lifetime," she says looking over to her endearing parents who were holding on to each other and looking at her lovingly.

"I am told that I may not remember any of you or anything about my time here after midnight. I find that hard to believe because each and every one of you are unforgettable and I just can't believe that there is a power on this earth that is strong enough to wipe out such an incredible experience.

So, I want to again say to each of you, continue to make the decisions that are true to who you are, what you believe in, and what you work hard to achieve. Because being true to oneself has to be the foundation that everything else that is accomplished in life depends on.

Sometimes making wrong decisions and having regrets build character. But when life throws you opportunities, you will have to reach up and catch the ones that keep you true to who you are and what you have worked for and allow what you don't catch to be a blessing and an opportunity for someone else equally deserving."

Kristina paused, panning the area and looked into the crowd at every face, then inhaled deeply after locking watery eyes with Marvin Lee's equally glassy stare.

"So, without regret, I sadly have to say goodbye to dreams that I once thought were important. I mean they still are, but someone who is not connected to Jolly now has an opportunity to seize the Hollywood life and medical advancement that I once looked forward to. I, Dr. Kristina Rosario, choose to stay here with all of you and accept the duties as your new Essence. I vow to work hard on your behalf and the behalf of the land. And with that said, as my first official duty, may I present to you your new designated protector of Essence."

The crowd cheered. Marvin Lee along with the tribesmen and elders who stood near the spirit teepee made their way through crowd openings, to the large fire pit near the podium area in a celebratory dance as the drums began to play again.

Kristina left the villagers to enjoy their celebration, but not before Marvin Lee and her eyes briefly caught each other again. Titus closed the car door. Kristina joined her parents and best friend for a ride back to her new home, Mistletoe Manor.

CHAPTER TWELVE

THE 7TH DAY OF ESSENCE

After taking the longer scenic route through Main Street, Kristina and her guests were amazed by the final look. The vibrant lights and decorative displays were appreciated by the amount of foot traffic of locals and tourists who were as wowed by the sights, sounds, and scents as they were.

Through the car's window, the passengers could see that the ice-skating rink was an added success for the downtown flare. The charm of the old-fashioned ice playground was enjoyed by the cautious beginners, the couples' arm in arm, and the more polished skaters performing sequences of upright, sit, and camel spins.

As the car approached the Ski Lodge, each passenger pointed out their favorite illuminated feature before being dropped off at the event space for the Gala. Kristina approved of the first impression. The larger-than-life nutcrackers outside at the entry were more than visually appealing. It was giving pre-anticipation.

Guests arriving in one-horse open sleighs was such a whimsical touch compared to the line of limousines at social events in Hollywood.

Ball Gowns and Tuxedos were the attire for the night, and the guests all presented in holiday elegance. Even the St. Bernard pups in the lobby had on little black bow ties.

Kristina's family joined her on the red carpet for photographs before kissing them on the cheek and waving at them as they continued into the banquet hall to give others a chance to photograph with her.

All of the chefs for the resort, Mistletoe Manor and the celebrity chefs relished the opportunity to get their picture taken with Essence Kristina and hurried back to the kitchen to complete preparations for the event. The aromas of rich sauces and gravies invaded nostrils and triggered cravings of hunger among the ensemble of cheerful and charitable guests.

Kristina was as delighted to see Dr. Isaiah Kennedy, Chief of Staff of her hospital and several of her coworkers as they were to see her. They all agreed that this was a monumental and worthy charity event and thanked her for the invitation and assured her that she would be missed and difficult to replace. In fact, they all made light of the fact that a departure was not exactly what was meant by the suggestion that she take some well-deserved time off to smell the proverbial roses.

She waved at the cast of Practicing Hollywood and the network executives who were on the red carpet doing what they do best; posing for likes and storylines and to outshine one another. Kristina walked away laughing within and could no longer imagine that she was missing from that group shot.

Kristina caught a glimpse of herself in a full-length mirror before the door of the hall. She loved the crystal beading on her champagne-gold strapless gown. As she took her final look of admiration, she gasped at the reflection of Marvin Lee who walked up behind her. She thought that he looked like a model who fell off the cover of a fashion magazine in his black tuxedo with his hair tied back in a tight man bun. She closed her eyes and inhaled his cologne to enhance the state of dreaminess that she was experiencing.

"I have never seen a more beautiful sight in my life," he said, staring at their reflections in the mirror. Kristina again was tongue paralyzed.

"So, Essence, is this always going to be your response when you see me?" he asked in a charming manner.

"I'm not quite sure yet. Ask me later."

Marvin Lee extended his arm to escort her into the banquet hall. A ray of applause rang out when Kristina entered the room. Simultaneously, her breathing literally stopped at first sight. Marvin Lee caught her as she lost her balance and strength to stand on her own. The winter wonderland decor was beyond enchanting. It was apparent that she was actually inside of the five snow globes combined.

She looked over at her mother who she knew had a big hand in every detail that she saw. Her parents looked on proudly with glassy eyes. The crystal snowflake and ice sickles to snow castle centerpieces and Christmas trees lent to its magical magnificence. The bouquet of Christmas roses at her table was indescribably spectacular.

The trumpets sounded catching the attention of everyone in the room. White curtains opened as music played. On stage were the children of Sugar Plum House who sang their rendition of "Feliz Navidad and We Wish You a Merry Christmas" just like they had rehearsed. The children cheered with glee as they were surprised at the end of their song when the magnanimous gingerbread house and gingerbread cake created by Mistletoe Manor's 3 talented chefs were rolled out and displayed.

As a surprise to Kristina, a large ice sculpture of a woman's open hand holding a glowing amber ball, was rolled out next. The crowded room chanted an array of wow responses before singing a group rendition of Happy Birthday, Dear Essence to her.

The band started to play, and guests began to gather on the dance floor where Kristina and Marvin stood. The two didn't exchange words but shared a look between them that lasted until they were both tapped on the shoulder by her parents.

"As much as your father and I hate to interrupt. We thought it was far past time that we were formally introduced to the gentleman who has captured the heart of our daughter."

"Mami!" she exclaimed under her breath, attempting to disguise embarrassment.

"Speak for yourself Delores, this fine young man and I met this morning while you ladies were doing whatever you had to do to make all of this possible. Marvin Lee and I had quite a long conversation," Kristina's father chimed in while placing one hand on his shoulder and a handshake greeting with the other. "I am going to steal my little Princessa away for a dance if you don't mind, young man."

"By all means Sir." Marvin Lee smiled and kissed Kristina's hand before releasing it to her father who threw a wink his way as if they shared information only between them.

Marvin Lee followed suit by asking Kristina's mother for a dance. They were both smiling. Mama Delores loved the song that the band was playing. London and Randall were both great ballroom dancers and took the dance floor by storm.

"So Papi, how do you really feel about all of this and my decision to stay? I know that it is a lot to take in."

"My Princessa. It is no less than I expected for your life. I knew from the start that you were destined for something amazing. Of course I didn't know at this magnitude, but it was your destiny. I am so grateful for the part that the universe allowed me to be a part of it."

"Are you sure that you and Mami won't reconsider and join me at the Manor. It is so much room, we would still have to call each other to get together," she joked. They laughed.

"Unfortunately, my dear, we both agree that you should start this part of your journey independent of us..."

"But Papi"

"No buts Mia. I suppose this must be how Mary and Joseph felt. We love you and will always support you as you continue on your path. We will visit as often as possible. Trust me, you couldn't keep your mother away from this level of Christmas decorating after this. And maybe one day when we retire, we will pick out a room or two...or three to get lost in if you will still have us."

"Of course I will. Mucho Gracias Papi,"

"Oh, Mia I almost forgot. Before I left the manor tonight, Rose asked me to give this to you," he said, while reaching into the inner pocket of his tuxedo jacket, pulling out a folded handkerchief, then handing it to her.

Kristina unfolded the handkerchief, that held a bitten, star-shaped Christmas cookie. Kristina smiled before taking a bite.

The magic of the night continued all the way until the last guest shook hands with Kristina.

Titus left an hour ago to take her parents back to the Manor, but Marvin Lee waited to be her driver for the night. He stood in the lobby holding her white furry shawl and matching hand muff. Kristina smiled at him, but before she could reach him, she noticed that Dr. Kennedy returned to the banquet hall because he had left his glasses behind on his table. He excitedly approached her and complimented her on his favorite part of the night.

"Oh, good you are still here! Dr. Rosario..."

"Kristina please", she replied.

"Kristina, I just have one question. How exactly were you able to create the illusion of Santa and the reindeer pulled sleigh lifting off from the lit helicopter pad. Now that is a trick that would be amazing at the hospital!

Kristina could only shrug her shoulders, smile and look over at Marvin Lee, because she did not have that on the agenda. Marvin Lee gave her a look of "I told you so."

CHAPTER THIRTEEN

1-Year Later

"Of course, London I am a little bummed that you can't make it up here this weekend, but I hope that you and Randall have a great time in Hawaii, and I will see you both at the Christmas Gala, right?"

"Tina, I wouldn't miss it for anything, I promise. When are your parents coming?"

"Girl, my mother actually stayed after Thanksgiving and has a whole nutcracker theme that is expected to be nothing short of amazing."

"I wouldn't expect anything less from Mama Delores"

"Oh, before I forget, Mya asked me to thank you again for all of your help. She is doing exceptionally well in the Midwifery program. We all are so proud of her."

"I was happy to help. And how is your hunky pie doing these days?"

"If you are referring to Marvin Lee, he should be back soon. He accompanied the Youth Camp counselors, and the staff of both the People Clinic and Pet Clinic to deliver care packages and perform wellness checks to some of the outskirt communities. They left on Dog sleds and snowmobiles! It was such a sight. I tell you girlfriend; it has never been a dull moment in Jolly since I arrived."

"Well until you tell me things have advanced to the next level with a hunk that shall remain nameless, I say things in Jolly could be a whole lot jollier."

"I have told you several times before, it is complicated."

"What is complicated?" interjected a soothing male voice entering the open door to her home office. Kristina smiled at the sight of Marvin Lee who was wearing a rather large smile and was clearly holding something behind his back.

"Okay Londy dear. I have to run."

"So, I hear," she laughed. "Carpe diem, sis."

"Love you too! Enjoy the beach and see you at the Gala," Kristina said to London, but stared into Marvin Lee's eyes. Then she hit the end call button on her cellphone.

"Welcome back. How was your trip? Kristina asked with a hint of nervousness in her voice.

"It was successful, but the best part is coming home. Especially since it's time to get the answer to the question that I asked you before I left."

"Yes, then there is that. You know Marvin Lee, I don't know if this has ever been done before. I mean is there a rule book for or against it?"

"I say, it shouldn't matter. Let's write our own rules. The Essence and The Protector. Our story. Our rule book. So again, and this time I am going to ask you to answer with your heart," he says as he bends to one knee and retrieves a ring from his shirt pocket. "Dr. Kristina Rosario, my Essence; will you throw fear, doubt, and caution to the wind and honor me by becoming my wife?"

"Dr. Marvin Lee Mass, Jr, my Protector; yes, I will be honored to be your wife and to have you as my husband," she replied with tears of joy as he placed the diamond ring upon her finger.

Their lips and hearts collided in an explosion with all self-appointed doubt, restrictions, and inhibition removed.

"You do know what this means now, don't you?"

"Um...I'm not sure what you mean," she smiled in wonder.

"You will officially be Dr. Kris Mass...Dr. Christmas." They both laughed and sealed it with another kiss.

Epilogue

The technology of man was temporarily suspended as the pitch-black sky remained still for eight minutes, cloaking the movement on the earth beneath its watch. The light echoes of footsteps against the cold pavement could not be heard by slumbering creatures of day or night during this time, nor could the sacred words that were spoken.

"May the Arctic winds carry my voice throughout the realm of life as it has for all those who spoke before me.

For when the soul of a child that descends from the heavens does not make it to Earth, it is captured by the Essence for supernatural rebirth and may be released into a host or unto the earth itself to be nurtured by love until their true destiny is revealed.

As the appointed Essence, I vow responsibility without conditions unselfishly to give all that is good, to preserve all that is good, and to give good back unto goodness."

At the precise moment that the stars returned to the sky to continue their duty of gaze, the lights of the city resumed without notice. The hem of a white fur-lined cape swept quickly across the ground, then vanished in the blink of an eye.

The muffled gurgling sounds of a baby awakened the silent night. The exterior porch light came on, illuminating the doorsteps of a quiet home to reveal a woven straw basket covered in a black and red buffalo checkered blanket with a glowing object shaped like a baby's rattle is seen by the surprised couple who looked in all directions for the deliverer before taking it inside.

The End

ACKNOWLEDGEMENT

Firstly, I give all honor to my Heavenly Father who has gifted me with the ability to write and spread joy with the power of my pen.

Next, I am extremely thankful to my family, my extended family and my close friends who are an extension of me. Thank you all for ALWAYS being supportive of my dream.

Lastly, but certainly far from least, my extremely talented group of Clubhouse Roommates whom I love dearly with all of my heart. I spend endless hours each and every day dwelling in their positive energy of creativity and am truly blessed that they are apart of my life's journey.

WHEN ONE OF US WIN, WE ALL WIN...
HAPPY WRITING ROOMIES!

ABOUT THE AUTHOR

E G Fahie

Credited with writing 4 Gospel stage play productions, and 4 published novellas to date. This faith-based author and freelance editor is a Washington D.C. native who discovered her love for writing in college while studying to become a Registered Nurse.

She combines the love of her craft with her successful medical career at the table in several writer rooms as a writer, story consultant, and set designer with a Los Angeles based media production company. She also co-hosts a daily online writing forum to inspire and encourage new and experienced writers of all genres.

Proclaiming that wife, mother, and grandmother are her favorite titles, she understands the meaning of true dedication, which translates across the pages of her work, welcoming the reader into the lives of her characters.

BOOKS BY THIS AUTHOR

After The Mud Season

Maintaining relationships prove to be challenging for a group of late iGen professionals attempting to carve their mark in Boston's prominent social and business community.

When circumstances and outside forces prove their inability to withstand the complexity of ego and heartbreak, the beautiful and brilliant tech savvy Renee Brown and former playboy and restaurateur, Phillip Mathews are forced to end their engagement and an 8-year relationship.

The legal battle that follows this power couple's break-up is brutal. The scars from social media and tabloid justice run deep leaving a trail of casualties and unhealed wounds forcing their close-knit circle of friends to choose sides of loyalty, ultimately forging an unlikely alliance to neutralize a common enemy.

Echoes From Half Quater-Hill

Echoes from Half-Quater Hill is the intertwining tale of the After and the Before of its companion novella, After the Mud Season.

Boston's star-crossed newlyweds, Phillip and Renee Mathews find themselves pulled apart once again by the enemy that they once thought had been neutralized.

Now the chase is on requiring the aid of both old and new friends to escape the clutches of what history reveals was bred in darkness in the pages of this cosmopolitan romance-suspense novella.

Percipience

In this contemporary modern magic novella, readers become deeply immersed in every page. Meghan Nicholson and Shakala Johnson are two feuding neighbors who inadvertently unleash a century-old curse that binds their fates in the most unimaginable way.

Overnight, they find themselves trapped in each other's bodies, visible to the world and to themselves reflected in mirrors as their rival, while their true identities are only seen through their naked eyes upon each other.

Clueless of the cause or how to reverse the spell, these unwilling partners are thrust into a race against time. As they struggle to maintain their separate lives, they are forced to work together and confront their deep-seeded prejudices and shatter long-held stereotypes.

Each day brings new challenges as they navigate unfamiliar worlds, grappling with the other's personal demons and hidden struggles.

www.ingramcontent.com/pod-product-compliance
Lightning Source LLC
Chambersburg PA
CBHW060753180626
46818CB00002B/557